THREE BOOKS

FOR JANE AND JOE

THREE BOOKS

HOUSEBOAT DAYS

SHADOW TRAIN

A WAVE

POEMS BY

JOHN ASHBERY

PENGUIN BOOKS

PENGUIN BOOKS
Published by the Penguin Group
Penguin Books USA Inc., 375 Hudson Street,
New York, New York 10014, U.S.A.
Penguin Books Ltd, 27 Wrights Lane,
London W8 5TZ, England
Penguin Books Australia Ltd, Ringwood, Victoria, Australia
Penguin Books Canada Ltd, 10 Alcorn Avenue,
Toronto, Ontario, Canada M4V 3B2
Penguin Books (N.Z.) Ltd, 182–190 Wairau Road, Auckland 10, New Zealand

Penguin Books Ltd, Registered Offices:
Harmondsworth, Middlesex, England

Houseboat Days first published in the United States of America in hardcover and paperback editions by The Viking Press and Penguin Books 1977

Shadow Train first published in the United States of America in hardcover and paperback editions by The Viking Press and Penguin Books 1981

A Wave first published in the United States of America by The Viking Press 1984
Published in Penguin Books 1985

First published in one volume in Penguin Books as *Three Books* 1993

10 9 8 7 6 5 4 3 2 1

Page 232 constitutes an extension to this copyright page.

LIBRARY OF CONGRESS CATALOGING IN PUBLICATION DATA
Ashbery, John.
[Poems. Selections]
Three books : poems / by John Ashbery.
p. cm.
Contents : Houseboat days—Shadow train—A wave.
ISBN 0 14 058.702 0
I. Title.
PS3501.S475A6 1993
811'.54—dc20 92-33956

Printed in the United States of America
Set in Garamond 3
Designed by Ann Gold

CONTENTS

HOUSEBOAT DAYS

SHADOW TRAIN

HOUSEBOAT DAYS

STREET MUSICIANS

One died, and the soul was wrenched out
Of the other in life, who, walking the streets
Wrapped in an identity like a coat, sees on and on
The same corners, volumetrics, shadows
Under trees. Farther than anyone was ever
Called, through increasingly suburban airs
And ways, with autumn falling over everything:
The plush leaves the chattels in barrels
Of an obscure family being evicted
Into the way it was, and is. The other beached
Glimpses of what the other was up to:
Revelations at last. So they grew to hate and forget each other.

So I cradle this average violin that knows
Only forgotten showtunes, but argues
The possibility of free declamation anchored
To a dull refrain, the year turning over on itself
In November, with the spaces among the days
More literal, the meat more visible on the bone.
Our question of a place of origin hangs
Like smoke: how we picnicked in pine forests,
In coves with the water always seeping up, and left
Our trash, sperm and excrement everywhere, smeared
On the landscape, to make of us what we could.

THE OTHER TRADITION

They all came, some wore sentiments
Emblazoned on T-shirts, proclaiming the lateness
Of the hour, and indeed the sun slanted its rays
Through branches of Norfolk Island pine as though
Politely clearing its throat, and all ideas settled
In a fuzz of dust under trees when it's drizzling:
The endless games of Scrabble, the boosters,
The celebrated omelette au Cantal, and through it
The roar of time plunging unchecked through the sluices
Of the days, dragging every sexual moment of it
Past the lenses: the end of something.
Only then did you glance up from your book,
Unable to comprehend what had been taking place, or
Say what you had been reading. More chairs
Were brought, and lamps were lit, but it tells
Nothing of how all this proceeded to materialize
Before you and the people waiting outside and in the next
Street, repeating its name over and over, until silence
Moved halfway up the darkened trunks,
And the meeting was called to order.

I still remember
How they found you, after a dream, in your thimble hat,
Studious as a butterfly in a parking lot.
The road home was nicer then. Dispersing, each of the
Troubadours had something to say about how charity
Had run its race and won, leaving you the ex-president
Of the event, and how, though many of those present
Had wished something to come of it, if only a distant
Wisp of smoke, yet none was so deceived as to hanker
After that cool non-being of just a few minutes before,
Now that the idea of a forest had clamped itself
Over the minutiae of the scene. You found this
Charming, but turned your face fully toward night,

Speaking into it like a megaphone, not hearing
Or caring, although these still live and are generous
And all ways contained, allowed to come and go
Indefinitely in and out of the stockade
They have so much trouble remembering, when your forgetting
Rescues them at last, as a star absorbs the night.

VARIANT

Sometimes a word will start it, like
Hands and feet, sun and gloves. The way
Is fraught with danger, you say, and I
Notice the word "fraught" as you are telling
Me about huge secret valleys some distance from
The mired fighting—"but always, lightly wooded
As they are, more deeply involved with the outcome
That will someday paste a black, bleeding label
In the sky, but until then
The echo, flowing freely in corridors, alleys,
And tame, surprised places far from anywhere,
Will be automatically locked out—*vox*
Clamans—do you see? End of tomorrow.
Don't try to start the car or look deeper
Into the eternal wimpling of the sky: luster
On luster, transparency floated onto the topmost layer
Until the whole thing overflows like a silver
Wedding cake or Christmas tree, in a cascade of tears."

COLLECTIVE DAWNS

You can have whatever you want.
Own it, I mean. In the sense
Of twisting it to you, through long, spiralling afternoons.
It has a sense beyond that meaning that was dropped there
And left to rot. The glacier seems

Impervious but is all shot through
With amethyst and the loud, distraught notes of the cuckoo.
They say the town is coming apart.
And people go around with a fragment of a smile
Missing from their faces. Life is getting cheaper

In some senses. Over the tops of old hills
The sunset jabs down, angled in a way it couldn't have
Been before. The bird-sellers walk back into it.
"We needn't fire their kilns; tonight is the epic
Night of the world. Grettir is coming back to us.
His severed hand has grabbed the short sword
And jumped back onto his wrist. The whole man is waking up.
The island is becoming a sun. Wait by this
Mistletoe bush and you will get the feeling of really
Being out of the world and with it. The sun
Is now an inlet of freshness whose very nature
Causes it to dry up." The old poems
In the book have changed value once again. Their black letter
Fools only themselves into ignoring their stiff, formal qualities,
  and they move
Insatiably out of reach of bathos and the bad line
Into a weird ether of forgotten dismemberments. Was it
This rosebud? Who said that?
The time of all forgotten
Things is at hand.

Therefore I write you
This bread and butter letter, you my friend
Who saved me from the mill pond of chill doubt
As to my own viability, and from the proud village
Of bourgeois comfort and despair, the mirrored spectacles of grief.
Let who can take courage from the dawn's
Coming up with the same idiot solution under another guise
So that all meanings should be scrambled this way
No matter how important they were to the men
Coming in the future, since this is the way it has to happen
For all things under the shrinking light to change
And the pattern to follow them, unheeded, bargained for
As it too is absorbed. But the guesswork
Has been taken out of millions of nights. The gasworks
Know it and fall to the ground, though no doom
Says it through the long cool hours of rest
While it sleeps as it can, as in fact it must, for the man to
find himself.

WOODEN BUILDINGS

The tests are good. You need a million of them.
You'd die laughing as I write to you
Through leaves and articulations, yes, laughing
Myself silly too. The funniest little thing . . .

That's how it all began. Looking back on it,
I wonder now if it could have been on some day
Findable in an old calendar? But no,
It wasn't out of history, but inside it.
That's the thing. On whatever day we came
To a small house built just above the water,
You had to stoop over to see inside the attic window.
Someone had judged the height to be just right
The way the light came in, and they are
Giving that party, to turn on that dishwasher
And we may be led, then, upward through more
Powerful forms of poetry, past columns
With peeling posters on them, to the country of indifference.
Meanwhile if the swell diapasons, blooms
Unhappily and too soon, the little people are nonetheless real.

PYROGRAPHY

Out here on Cottage Grove it matters. The galloping
Wind balks at its shadow. The carriages
Are drawn forward under a sky of fumed oak.
This is America calling:
The mirroring of state to state,
Of voice to voice on the wires,
The force of colloquial greetings like golden
Pollen sinking on the afternoon breeze.
In service stairs the sweet corruption thrives;
The page of dusk turns like a creaking revolving stage in
 Warren, Ohio.

If this is the way it is let's leave,
They agree, and soon the slow boxcar journey begins,
Gradually accelerating until the gyrating fans of suburbs
Enfolding the darkness of cities are remembered
Only as a recurring tic. And midway
We meet the disappointed, returning ones, without its
Being able to stop us in the headlong night
Toward the nothing of the coast. At Bolinas
The houses doze and seem to wonder why through the
Pacific haze, and the dreams alternately glow and grow dull.
Why be hanging on here? Like kites, circling,
Slipping on a ramp of air, but always circling?

But the variable cloudiness is pouring it on,
Flooding back to you like the meaning of a joke,
The land wasn't immediately appealing, we built it
Partly over with fake ruins, in the image of ourselves:
An arch that terminates in mid-keystone, a crumbling stone pier
For laundresses, an open-air theater, never completed
And only partially designed. How are we to inhabit
This space from which the fourth wall is invariably missing,

As in a stage-set or dollhouse, except by staying as we are,
In lost profile, facing the stars, with dozens of as yet
Unrealized projects, and a strict sense
Of time running out, of evening presenting
The tactfully folded-over bill? And we fit
Rather too easily into it, become transparent,
Almost ghosts. One day
The birds and animals in the pasture have absorbed
The color, the density of the surroundings,
The leaves are alive, and too heavy with life.

A long period of adjustment followed.
In the cities at the turn of the century they knew about it
But were careful not to let on as the iceman and the milkman
Disappeared down the block and the postman shouted
His daily rounds. The children under the trees knew it
But all the fathers returning home
On streetcars after a satisfying day at the office undid it:
The climate was still floral and all the wallpaper
In a million homes all over the land conspired to hide it.
One day we thought of painted furniture, of how
It just slightly changes everything in the room
And in the yard outside, and how, if we were going
To be able to write the history of our time, starting with today,
It would be necessary to model all these unimportant details
So as to be able to include them; otherwise the narrative
Would have that flat, sandpapered look the sky gets
Out in the middle west toward the end of summer,
The look of wanting to back out before the argument
Has been resolved, and at the same time to save appearances
So that tomorrow will be pure. Therefore, since we have to do
our business
In spite of things, why not make it in spite of everything?

That way, maybe the feeble lakes and swamps
Of the back country will get plugged into the circuit
And not just the major events but the whole incredible
Mass of everything happening simultaneously and pairing off,
Channeling itself into history, will unroll
As carefully and as casually as a conversation in the next room,
And the purity of today will invest us like a breeze,
Only be hard, spare, ironical: something one can
Tip one's hat to and still get some use out of.

The parade is turning into our street.
My stars, the burnished uniforms and prismatic
Features of this instant belong here. The land
Is pulling away from the magic, glittering coastal towns
To an aforementioned rendezvous with August and December.
The hunch is it will always be this way,
The look, the way things first scared you
In the night light, and later turned out to be,
Yet still capable, all the same, of a narrow fidelity
To what you and they wanted to become:
No sighs like Russian music, only a vast unravelling
Out toward the junctions and to the darkness beyond
To these bare fields, built at today's expense.

THE GAZING GRAIN

The tires slowly came to a rubbery stop.
Alliterative festoons in the sky noted
That this branchy birthplace of presidents was also
The big frigidaire-cum-cowbarn where mendicant

And margrave alike waited out the results
Of the natural elections. So any openness of song
Was the plainer way. O take me to the banks
Of your Mississippi over there, etc. Like a plant

Rooted in parched earth I am
A stranger myself in the dramatic lighting,
The result of war. That which is given to see
At any moment is the residue, shadowed

In gold or emerging into the clear bluish haze
Of uncertainty. We come back to ourselves
Through the rubbish of cloud and tree-spattered pavement.
These days stand like vapor under the trees.

UNCTUOUS PLATITUDES

There is no reason for the surcharge to bother you.
Living in a city one is nonplussed by some

Of the inhabitants. The weather has grown gray with age.
Poltergeists go about their business, sometimes

Demanding a sweeping revision. The breath of the air
Is invisible. People stay

Next to the edges of fields, hoping that out of nothing
Something will come, and it does, but what? Embers

Of the rain tamp down the shitty darkness that issues
From nowhere. A man in her room, you say.

I like the really wonderful way you express things
So that it might be said, that of all the ways in which to

Emphasize a posture or a particular mental climate
Like this gray-violet one with a thin white irregular line

Descending the two vertical sides, these are those which
Can also unsay an infinite number of pauses

In the ceramic day. Every invitation
To every stranger is met at the station.

THE COUPLE IN THE NEXT ROOM

She liked the blue drapes. They made a star
At the angle. A boy in leather moved in.
Later they found names from the turn of the century
Coming home one evening. The whole of being
Unknown absorbed into the stalk. A free
Bride on the rails warning to notice other
Hers and the great graves that outwore them
Like faces on a building, the lightning rod
Of a name calibrated all their musing differences.

Another day. Deliberations are recessed
In an iron-blue chamber of that afternoon
On which we wore things and looked well at
A slab of business rising behind the stars.

THE EXPLANATION

The luxury of now is that the cancelled gala has been
Put back in. The orchestra is starting to tune up.
The tone-row of a dripping faucet is batted back and forth
Among the kitchen, the confusion outside, the pale bluster
Of the sky, the correct but insidious grass.
The conductor, a glass of water, permits all kinds
Of wacky analogies to glance off him, and, circling outward,
To bring in the night. Nothing is too "unimportant"
Or too important, for that matter. The newspaper and the garbage
Wrapped in it, the over, the under.
You get thrown to one side
Into a kind of broom closet as the argument continues carolling
Ideas from the novel of which this is the unsuccessful
Stage adaptation. Too much, perhaps, gets lost.
What about arriving after sunset on the beach of a
Dank but extremely beautiful island to hear the speeches
Of the invisible natives, whose punishment is speech?

At the top of his teddy-bear throne, the ruler,
Still lit by the sun, gazes blankly across at something
Opposite. His eyes are empty rectangles, shaped
Like slightly curved sticks of chewing gum. He witnesses.
But we are the witnesses.

In the increasingly convincing darkness
The words become palpable, like a fruit
That is too beautiful to eat. We want these
Down here on our level. But the tedium persists
In the form of remarks exchanged by birds
Before the curtain. What am I doing up here?
Pretending to resist but secretly giving in so as to reappear
In a completely new outfit and group of colors once today's
Bandage has been removed, is all.

LOVING MAD TOM

You thought it was wrong. And afterwards
When everyone had gone out, their lying persisted in your ears,
Across the water. You didn't see the miserable dawns piled up,
One after the other, stretching away. Their word only
Waited for you like the truth, and sometimes
Out of a pure, unintentional song, the meaning
Stammered nonetheless, and your zeal could see
To the opposite shore, where it was all coming true.

Then to lay it down like a load
And take up the dream stitching again, as though
It were still old, as on a bright, unseasonably cold
Afternoon, is a dream past living. Best to leave it there
And quickly tiptoe out. The music ended anyway. The occasions
In your arms went along with it and seemed
To supply the necessary sense. But like
A farmhouse in the city, on some busy, deserted metropolitan avenue,
It was all too much in the way it fell silent,
Forewarned, as though an invisible face looked out
From hooded windows, as the rain suddenly starts to fall
And the lightning goes crazy, and the thunder faints dead away.
That was a way of getting here,
He thought. A spear of fire, a horse of air,
And the rest is done for you, to go with the rest,
To match up with everything accomplished until now.
And always one stream is pointing north
To reeds and leaves, and the stunned land
Flowers in dejection. This station in the woods,
How was it built? This place
Of communicating back along the way, all the way back?
And in an orgy of minutes the waiting
Seeks to continue, to begin again,
Amid bugs, the barking of dogs, all the
Maddening irregularities of trees, and night falls anyway.

BUSINESS PERSONALS

The disquieting muses again: what are "leftovers"?
Perhaps they have names for it all, who come bearing
Worn signs of privilege whose authority
Speaks out of the accumulation of age and faded colors
To the center of today. Floating heart, why
Wander on senselessly? The tall guardians
Of yesterday are steep as cliff shadows;
Whatever path you take abounds in their sense.
All presently lead downward, to the harbor view.

Therefore do your knees need to be made strong, by running.
We have places for the training and a special on equipment:
Knee-pads, balancing poles and the rest. It works
In the sense of aging: you come out always a little ahead
And not so far as to lose a sense of the crowd
Of disciples. That were tyranny,
Outrage, hubris. Meanwhile this tent is silence
Itself. Its walls are opaque, so as not to see
The road; a pleasant, half-heard melody climbs to its ceiling—
Not peace, but rest the doctor ordered. Tomorrow . . .
And songs climb out of the flames of the near campfires,
Pale, pastel things exquisite in their frailness
With a note or two to indicate it isn't lost,
On them at least. The songs decorate our notion of the world
And mark its limits, like a frieze of soap-bubbles.

What caused us to start caring?
In the beginning was only sedge, a field of water
Wrinkled by the wind. Slowly
The trees increased the novelty of always being alone,
The rest began to be sketched in, and then . . . silence,
Or blankness, for a number of years. Could one return
To the idea of nature summed up in these pastoral images?

Yet the present has done its work of building
A rampart against the past, not a rampart,
A barbed-wire fence. So now we know
What occupations to stick to (scrimshaw, spinning tall tales)
By the way the songs deepen the color of the shadow
Impregnating your hobby as you bend over it,
Squinting. I could make a list
Of each one of my possessions and the direction it
Pointed in, how much each thing cost, how much for wood, string,
colored ink, etc.

The song makes no mention of directions.
At most it twists the longitude lines overhead
Like twigs to form a crude shelter. (The ship
Hasn't arrived, it was only a dream. It's somewhere near
Cape Horn, despite all the efforts of Boreas to puff out
Those drooping sails.) The idea of great distance
Is permitted, even implicit in the slow dripping
Of a lute. How to get out?
This giant will never let us out unless we blind him.

And that's how, one day, I got home.
Don't be shocked that the old walls
Hang in rags now, that the rainbow has hardened
Into a permanent late afternoon that elicits too-long
Shadows and indiscretions from the bottom
Of the soul. Such simple things,
And we make of them something so complex it defeats us,
Almost. Why can't everything be simple again,
Like the first words of the first song as they occurred
To one who, rapt, wrote them down and later sang them:
"Only danger deflects
The arrow from the center of the persimmon disc,

Its final resting place. And should you be addressing yourself
To danger? When it takes the form of bleachers
Sparsely occupied by an audience which has
Already witnessed the events of which you write,
Tellingly, in your log? Properly acknowledged
It will dissipate like the pale pink and blue handkerchiefs
That vanished centuries ago into the blue dome
That surrounds us, but which are, some maintain, still here."

CRAZY WEATHER

It's this crazy weather we've been having:
Falling forward one minute, lying down the next
Among the loose grasses and soft, white, nameless flowers.
People have been making a garment out of it,
Stitching the white of lilacs together with lightning
At some anonymous crossroads. The sky calls
To the deaf earth. The proverbial disarray
Of morning corrects itself as you stand up.
You are wearing a text. The lines
Droop to your shoelaces and I shall never want or need
Any other literature than this poetry of mud
And ambitious reminiscences of times when it came easily
Through the then woods and ploughed fields and had
A simple unconscious dignity we can never hope to
Approximate now except in narrow ravines nobody
Will inspect where some late sample of the rare,
Uninteresting specimen might still be putting out shoots,
 for all we know.

ON THE TOWPATH

At the sign "Fred Muffin's Antiques" they turned off the
road into a narrow lane lined with shabby houses.

If the thirst would subside just for awhile
It would be a little bit, enough.
This has happened.
The insipid chiming of the seconds
Has given way to an arc of silence
So old it had never ceased to exist
On the roofs of buildings, in the sky.

The ground is tentative.
The pygmies and jacaranda that were here yesterday
Are back today, only less so.
It is a barrier of fact
Shielding the sky from the earth.

On the earth a many-colored tower of longing rises.
There are many ads (to help pay for all this).
Something interesting is happening on every landing.
Ladies of the Second Empire gotten up as characters from Perrault:
Red Riding Hood, Cinderella, the Sleeping Beauty,
Are silhouetted against the stained-glass windows.
A white figure runs to the edge of some rampart
In a hurry only to observe the distance,
And having done so, drops back into the mass
Of clock-faces, spires, stalactite machicolations.
It was the walking sideways, visible from far away,
That told what it was to be known
And kept, as a secret is known and kept.

The sun fades like the spreading
Of a peacock's tail, as though twilight

Might be read as a warning to those desperate
For easy solutions. This scalp of night
Doesn't continue or break off the vacuous chatter
That went on, off and on, all day:
That there could be rain, and
That it could be like lines, ruled lines scored
Across the garden of violet cabbages,
That these and other things could stay on
Longer, though not forever of course;
That other commensals might replace them
And leave in their turn. No,

We aren't meaning that any more.
The question has been asked
As though an immense natural bridge had been
Strung across the landscape to any point you wanted.
The ellipse is as aimless as that,
Stretching invisibly into the future so as to reappear
In our present. Its flexing is its account,
Return to the point of no return.

MELODIC TRAINS

A little girl with scarlet enameled fingernails
Asks me what time it is—evidently that's a toy wristwatch
She's wearing, for fun. And it is fun to wear other
Odd things, like this briar pipe and tweed coat

Like date-colored sierras with the lines of seams
Sketched in and plunging now and then into unfathomable
Valleys that can't be deduced by the shape of the person
Sitting inside it—me, and just as our way is flat across
Dales and gulches, as though our train were a pencil

Guided by a ruler held against a photomural of the Alps
We both come to see distance as something unofficial
And impersonal yet not without its curious justification
Like the time of a stopped watch—right twice a day.

Only the wait in stations is vague and
Dimensionless, like oneself. How do they decide how much
Time to spend in each? One begins to suspect there's no
Rule or that it's applied haphazardly.

Sadness of the faces of children on the platform,
Concern of the grownups for connections, for the chances
Of getting a taxi, since these have no timetable.
You get one if you can find one though in principle

You can always find one, but the segment of chance
In the circle of certainty is what gives these leaning
Tower of Pisa figures their aspect of dogged
Impatience, banking forward into the wind.

In short any stop before the final one creates
Clouds of anxiety, of sad, regretful impatience

With ourselves, our lives, the way we have been dealing
With other people up until now. Why couldn't
We have been more considerate? These figures leaving

The platform or waiting to board the train are my brothers
In a way that really wants to tell me why there is so little
Panic and disorder in the world, and so much unhappiness.
If I were to get down now to stretch, take a few steps

In the wearying and world-weary clouds of steam like great
White apples, might I just through proximity and aping
Of postures and attitudes communicate this concern of mine
To them? That their jagged attitudes correspond to mine,

That their beefing strikes answering silver bells within
My own chest, and that I know, as they do, how the last
Stop is the most anxious one of all, though it means
Getting home at last, to the pleasures and dissatisfactions of home?

It's as though a visible chorus called up the different
Stages of the journey, singing about them and being them:
Not the people in the station, not the child opposite me
With currant fingernails, but the windows, seen through,

Reflecting imperfectly, ruthlessly splitting open the bluish
Vague landscape like a zipper. Each voice has its own
Descending scale to put one in one's place at every stage;
One need never not know where one is

Unless one give up listening, sleeping, approaching a small
Western town that is nothing but a windmill. Then
The great fury of the end can drop as the solo
Voices tell about it, wreathing it somehow with an aura

Of good fortune and colossal welcomes from the mayor and
Citizens' committees tossing their hats into the air.
To hear them singing you'd think it had already happened
And we had focused back on the furniture of the air.

BIRD'S-EYE VIEW
OF THE TOOL AND DIE CO.

For a long time I used to get up early.
20-30 vision, hemorrhoids intact, he checks into the
Enclosure of time familiarizing dreams
For better or worse. The edges rub off,
The slant gets lost. Whatever the villagers
Are celebrating with less conviction is
The less you. Index of own organ-music playing,
Machinations over the architecture (too
Light to make much of a dent) against meditated
Gang-wars, ice cream, loss, palm terrain.

Under and around the quick background
Surface is improvisation. The force of
Living hopelessly backward into a past of striped
Conversations. As long as none of them ends this side
Of the mirrored desert in terrorist chorales.
The finest car is as the simplest home off the coast
Of all small cliffs too short to be haze. You turn
To speak to someone beside the dock and the lighthouse
Shines like garnets. It has become a stricture.

WET CASEMENTS

When Edward Raban, coming along the passage,
walked into the open doorway, he saw that it
was raining. It was not raining much.
KAFKA, *WEDDING PREPARATIONS*
IN THE COUNTRY

The conception is interesting: to see, as though reflected
In streaming windowpanes, the look of others through
Their own eyes. A digest of their correct impressions of
Their self-analytical attitudes overlaid by your
Ghostly transparent face. You in falbalas
Of some distant but not too distant era, the cosmetics,
The shoes perfectly pointed, drifting (how long you
Have been drifting; how long I have too for that matter)
Like a bottle-imp toward a surface which can never be approached,
Never pierced through into the timeless energy of a present
Which would have its own opinions on these matters,
Are an epistemological snapshot of the processes
That first mentioned your name at some crowded cocktail
Party long ago, and someone (not the person addressed)
Overheard it and carried that name around in his wallet
For years as the wallet crumbled and bills slid in
And out of it. I want that information very much today,

Can't have it, and this makes me angry.
I shall use my anger to build a bridge like that
Of Avignon, on which people may dance for the feeling
Of dancing on a bridge. I shall at last see my complete face
Reflected not in the water but in the worn stone floor of my bridge.

I shall keep to myself.
I shall not repeat others' comments about me.

SAYING IT TO KEEP IT FROM HAPPENING

Some departure from the norm
Will occur as time grows more open about it.
The consensus gradually changed; nobody
Lies about it any more. Rust dark pouring
Over the body, changing it without decay—
People with too many things on their minds, but we live
In the interstices, between a vacant stare and the ceiling,
Our lives remind us. Finally this is consciousness
And the other livers of it get off at the same stop.
How careless. Yet in the end each of us
Is seen to have traveled the same distance—it's time
That counts, and how deeply you have invested in it,
Crossing the street of an event, as though coming out of it were
The same as making it happen. You're not sorry,
Of course, especially if this was the way it had to happen,
Yet would like an exacter share, something about time
That only a clock can tell you: how it feels, not what it means.
It is a long field, and we know only the far end of it,
Not the part we presumably had to go through to get there.
If it isn't enough, take the idea
Inherent in the day, armloads of wheat and flowers
Lying around flat on handtrucks, if maybe it means more
In pertaining to you, yet what is is what happens in the end
As though you cared. The event combined with
Beams leading up to it for the look of force adapted to the wiser
Usages of age, but it's both there
And not there, like washing or sawdust in the sunlight,
At the back of the mind, where we live now.

DAFFY DUCK IN HOLLYWOOD

Something strange is creeping across me.
La Celestina has only to warble the first few bars
Of "I Thought about You" or something mellow from
Amadigi di Gaula for everything—a mint-condition can
Of Rumford's Baking Powder, a celluloid earring, Speedy
Gonzales, the latest from Helen Topping Miller's fertile
Escritoire, a sheaf of suggestive pix on greige, deckle-edged
Stock—to come clattering through the rainbow trellis
Where Pistachio Avenue rams the 2300 block of Highland
Fling Terrace. He promised he'd get me out of this one,
That mean old cartoonist, but just look what he's
Done to me now! I scarce dare approach me mug's attenuated
Reflection in yon hubcap, so jaundiced, so *déconfit*
Are its lineaments—fun, no doubt, for some quack phrenologist's
Fern-clogged waiting room, but hardly what you'd call
Companionable. But everything is getting choked to the point of
Silence. Just now a magnetic storm hung in the swatch of sky
Over the Fudds' garage, reducing it—drastically—
To the aura of a plumbago-blue log cabin on
A Gadsden Purchase commemorative cover. Suddenly all is
Loathing. I don't want to go back inside any more. You meet
Enough vague people on this emerald traffic-island—no,
Not people, comings and goings, more: mutterings, splatterings,
The bizarrely but effectively equipped infantries of happy-go-nutty
Vegetal jacqueries, plumed, pointed at the little
White cardboard castle over the mill run. "Up
The lazy river, how happy we could be?"
How will it end? That geranium glow
Over Anaheim's had the riot act read to it by the
Etna-size firecracker that exploded last minute into
A *carte du Tendre* in whose lower right-hand corner
(Hard by the jock-itch sand-trap that skirts
The asparagus patch of algolagnic *nuits blanches*) Amadis

Is cozening the Princesse de Clèves into a midnight micturition spree
On the Tamigi with the Wallets (Walt, Blossom, and little
Skeezix) on a lamé barge "borrowed" from Ollie
Of the Movies' dread mistress of the robes. Wait!
I have an announcement! This wide, tepidly meandering,
Civilized Lethe (one can barely make out the maypoles
And *châlets de nécessité* on its sedgy shore) leads to Tophet, that
Landfill-haunted, not-so-residential resort from which
Some travellers return! This whole moment is the groin
Of a borborygmic giant who even now
Is rolling over on us in his sleep. Farewell bocages,
Tanneries, water-meadows. The allegory comes unsnarled
Too soon; a shower of pecky acajou harpoons is
About all there is to be noted between tornadoes. I have
Only my intermittent life in your thoughts to live
Which is like thinking in another language. Everything
Depends on whether somebody reminds you of me.
That this is a fabulation, and that those "other times"
Are in fact the silences of the soul, picked out in
Diamonds on stygian velvet, matters less than it should.
Prodigies of timing may be arranged to convince them
We live in one dimension, they in ours. While I
Abroad through all the coasts of dark destruction seek
Deliverance for us all, think in that language: its
Grammar, though tortured, offers pavilions
At each new parting of the ways. Pastel
Ambulances scoop up the quick and hie them to hospitals.
"It's all bits and pieces, spangles, patches, really; nothing
Stands alone. What happened to creative evolution?"
Sighed Aglavaine. Then to her Sélysette: "If his
Achievement is only to end up less boring than the others,
What's keeping us here? Why not leave at once?
I have to stay here while they sit in there,

Laugh, drink, have fine time. In my day
One lay under the tough green leaves,
Pretending not to notice how they bled into
The sky's aqua, the wafted-away no-color of regions supposed
Not to concern us. And so we too
Came where the others came: nights of physical endurance,
Or if, by day, our behavior was anarchically
Correct, at least by New Brutalism standards, all then
Grew taciturn by previous agreement. We were spirited
Away *en bateau*, under cover of fudge dark.
It's not the incomplete importunes, but the spookiness
Of the finished product. True, to ask less were folly, yet
If he is the result of himself, how much the better
For him we ought to be! And how little, finally,
We take this into account! Is the puckered garance satin
Of a case that once held a brace of dueling pistols our
Only acknowledging of that color? I like not this,
Methinks, yet this disappointing sequel to ourselves
Has been applauded in London and St. Petersburg. Somewhere
Ravens pray for us."

The storm finished brewing. And thus
She questioned all who came in at the great gate, but none
She found who ever heard of Amadis,
Nor of stern Aureng-Zebe, his first love. Some
There were to whom this mattered not a jot: since all
By definition is completeness (so
In utter darkness they reasoned), why not
Accept it as it pleases to reveal itself? As when
Low skyscrapers from lower-hanging clouds reveal
A turret there, an art-deco escarpment here, and last perhaps
The pattern that may carry the sense, but
Stays hidden in the mysteries of pagination.
Not what we see but how we see it matters; all's

Alike, the same, and we greet him who announces
The change as we would greet the change itself.
All life is but a figment; conversely, the tiny
Tome that slips from your hand is not perhaps the
Missing link in this invisible picnic whose leverage
Shrouds our sense of it. Therefore bivouac we
On this great, blond highway, unimpeded by
Veiled scruples, worn conundrums. Morning is
Impermanent. Grab sex things, swing up
Over the horizon like a boy
On a fishing expedition. No one really knows
Or cares whether this is the whole of which parts
Were vouchsafed—once—but to be ambling on's
The tradition more than the safekeeping of it. This mulch for
Play keeps them interested and busy while the big,
Vaguer stuff can decide what it wants—what maps, what
Model cities, how much waste space. Life, our
Life anyway, is between. We don't mind
Or notice any more that the sky *is* green, a parrot
One, but have our earnest where it chances on us,
Disingenuous, intrigued, inviting more,
Always invoking the echo, a summer's day.

ALL KINDS OF CARESSES

The code-name losses and compensations
Float in and around us through the window.
It helps to know what direction the body comes from.
It isn't absolutely clear. In words
Bitter as a field of mustard we
Copy certain parts, then decline them.
These are not only gestures: they imply
Complex relations with one another. Sometimes one
Stays on for a while, a trace of lamp black
In a room full of gray furniture.

I now know all there is to know
About my body. I know too the direction
My feet are pointed in. For the time being
It is enough to suspend judgment, by which I don't mean
Forever, since judgment is also a storm, i.e., from
Somewhere else, sinking pleasure craft at moorings,
Looking, kicking in the sky.

Try to move with these hard blues,
These harsh yellows, these hands and feet.
Our gestures have taken us farther into the day
Than tomorrow will understand.

They live us. And we understand them when they sing,
Long after the perfume has worn off.
In the night the eye chisels a new phantom.

LOST AND FOUND AND LOST AGAIN

Like an object whose loss has begun to be felt
Though not yet noticed, your pulsar signals
To the present death. "*It must be cold out on the river*
Today." "You could make sweet ones on earth."

They tell him nothing. And the neon Bodoni
Presses its invitation to inspect the figures
Of this evening seeping from a far and fatal corridor
Of relaxed vigilance: these colors and this speech only.

TWO DEATHS

The lace
Of spoken breathing fades quite quickly, becomes
Something it has no part in, the chairs and
The mugs used by the new young tenants, whose glance
Is elsewhere. The body rounds out the muted
Magic, and sighs.
                                        Unkind to want
To be here, but the way back is cut off:
You can only stand and nod, exchange stares, but
The time of manners is going, the woodpile in the corner
Of the lot exudes the peace of the forest. Perennially,
We die and are taken up again. How is it
With us, we are asked, and the voice
On the old Edison cylinder tells it: obliquity,
The condition of straightness of these tutorials,
Firm when it is held in the hand.

He goes out.
The empty parlor is as big as a hill.

HOUSEBOAT DAYS

"The skin is broken. The hotel breakfast china
Poking ahead to the last week in August, not really
Very much at all, found the land where you began . . ."
The hills smouldered up blue that day, again
You walk five feet along the shore, and you duck
As a common heresy sweeps over. We can botanize
About this for centuries, and the little dazey
Blooms again in the cities. The mind
Is so hospitable, taking in everything
Like boarders, and you don't see until
It's all over how little there was to learn
Once the stench of knowledge has dissipated, and the trouvailles
Of every one of the senses fallen back. Really, he
Said, that insincerity of reasoning on behalf of one's
Sincere convictions, true or false in themselves
As the case may be, to which, if we are unwise enough
To argue at all with each other, we must be tempted
At times—do you see where it leads? To pain,
And the triumph over pain, still hidden
In these low-lying hills which rob us
Of all privacy, as though one were always about to meet
One's double through the chain of cigar smoke
And then it . . . happens, like an explosion in the brain,
Only it's a catastrophe on another planet to which
One has been invited, and as surely cannot refuse:
Pain in the cistern, in the gutters, and if we merely
Wait awhile, that denial, as though a universe of pain
Had been created just so as to deny its own existence.
But I don't set much stock in things
Beyond the weather and the certainties of living and dying:
The rest is optional. To praise this, blame that,
Leads one subtly away from the beginning, where

We must stay, in motion. To flash light
Into the house within, its many chambers,
Its memories and associations, upon its inscribed
And pictured walls, argues enough that life is various.
Life is beautiful. He who reads that
As in the window of some distant, speeding train
Knows what he wants, and what will befall.

Pinpricks of rain fall again.
And from across the quite wide median with its
Little white flowers, a reply is broadcast:
"Dissolve parliament. Hold new elections."
It would be deplorable if the rain also washed away
This profile at the window that moves, and moves on,
Knowing that it moves, and knows nothing else. It is the light
At the end of the tunnel as it might be seen
By him looking out somberly at the shower,
The picture of hope a dying man might turn away from,
Realizing that hope is something else, something concrete
You can't have. So, winding past certain pillars
Until you get to evening's malachite one, it becomes a vast dream
Of having that can topple governments, level towns and cities
With the pressure of sleep building up behind it.
The surge creates its own edge
And you must proceed this way: mornings of assent,
Indifferent noons leading to the ripple of the question
Of late afternoon projected into evening.
Arabesques and runnels are the result
Over the public address system, on the seismograph at Berkeley.
A little simple arithmetic tells you that to be with you
In this passage, this movement, is what the instance costs:
A sail out of some afternoon, beyond amazement, astonished,

Apparently not tampered with. As the rain gathers and protects
Its own darkness, the place in the slipcover is noticed
For the first and last time, fading like the spine
Of an adventure novel behind glass, behind the teacups.

WHETHER IT EXISTS

All through the fifties and sixties the land tilted
Toward the bowl of life. Now life
Has moved in that direction. We taste the conviction
Minus the rind, the pulp and the seeds. It
Goes down smoothly.

At a later date I added color
And the field became a shed in ways I no longer remember.
Familiarly, but without tenderness, the sunset pours its
Dance music on the (again) slanting barrens.
The problems we were speaking of move up toward them.

THE LAMENT UPON THE WATERS

For the disciple nothing had changed. The mood was still
Gray tolerance, as the road marched along
Singing its little song of despair. Once, a cry
Started up out of the hills. That old, puzzling persuasion

Again. Sex was part of this,
And the shock of day turning into night.
Though we always found something delicate (too delicate
For some tastes, perhaps) to touch, to desire.

And we made much of this sort of materiality
That clogged the weight of starlight, made it seem
Fibrous, yet there was a chance in this
To see the present as it never had existed,

Clear and shapeless, in an atmosphere like cut glass.
At Latour-Maubourg you said this was a good thing, and on the steps
Of Métro Jasmin the couriers nodded to us correctly, and the
Pact was sealed in the sky. But now moments surround us

Like a crowd, some inquisitive faces, some hostile ones,
Some engimatic or turned away to an anterior form of time
Given once and for all. The jetstream inscribes a final flourish
That melts as it stays. The problem isn't how to proceed

But is one of being: whether this ever was, and whose
It shall be. To be starting out, just one step
Off the sidewalk, and as such pulled back into the glittering
Snowstorm of stinging tentacles of how that would be worked out

If we ever work it out. And the voice came back at him
Across the water, rubbing it the wrong way: "Thou

Canst but undo the wrong thou hast done." The sackbuts
Embellish it, and we are never any closer to the collision

Of the waters, the peace of light drowning light,
Grabbing it, holding it up streaming. It is all one. It lies
All around, its new message, guilt, the admission
Of guilt, your new act. Time buys

The receiver, the onlooker of the earlier system, but cannot
Buy back the rest. It is night that fell
At the edge of your footsteps as the music stopped.
And we heard the bells for the first time. It is your chapter, I said.

DRAME BOURGEOIS

A sudden, acrid smell of roses, and the urchin
Turns away, tears level in the eyes. Waffled feeling:
"You'd scarce credit it, mum," as the starched
Moment of outline recedes down a corridor, some parts
Lighter, but the ensemble always darker as the vanishing point
Is reached and turns itself
Into an old army blanket, or something flat and material
As this idea of an old stump in a woods somewhere.
Then it is true. . . . It is you, who, that
Wet evening in March . . . Madam, say no more,
Your very lack of information is special to me,
Your emptying glance, prisms which I treasure up.
Only let your voice not become this clarion,
Alarum in the wilderness, calling me back to piety, to sense,
Else I am undone, for late haze drapes the golf links
And the gilded spines of these tomes blaze too bright.

AND *UT PICTURA POESIS* IS HER NAME

You can't say it that way any more.
Bothered about beauty you have to
Come out into the open, into a clearing,
And rest. Certainly whatever funny happens to you
Is OK. To demand more than this would be strange
Of you, you who have so many lovers,
People who look up to you and are willing
To do things for you, but you think
It's not right, that if they really knew you . . .
So much for self-analysis. Now,
About what to put in your poem-painting:
Flowers are always nice, particularly delphinium.
Names of boys you once knew and their sleds,
Skyrockets are good—do they still exist?
There are a lot of other things of the same quality
As those I've mentioned. Now one must
Find a few important words, and a lot of low-keyed,
Dull-sounding ones. She approached me
About buying her desk. Suddenly the street was
Bananas and the clangor of Japanese instruments.
Humdrum testaments were scattered around. His head
Locked into mine. We were a seesaw. Something
Ought to be written about how this affects
You when you write poetry:
The extreme austerity of an almost empty mind
Colliding with the lush, Rousseau-like foliage of its desire
to communicate
Something between breaths, if only for the sake
Of others and their desire to understand you and desert you
For other centers of communication, so that understanding
May begin, and in doing so be undone.

WHAT IS POETRY

The medieval town, with frieze
Of boy scouts from Nagoya? The snow

That came when we wanted it to snow?
Beautiful images? Trying to avoid

Ideas, as in this poem? But we
Go back to them as to a wife, leaving

The mistress we desire? Now they
Will have to believe it

As we believe it. In school
All the thought got combed out:

What was left was like a field.
Shut your eyes, and you can feel it for miles around.

Now open them on a thin vertical path.
It might give us—what?—some flowers soon?

AND OTHERS, VAGUER PRESENCES

Are built out of the meshing of life and space
At the point where we are wholly revealed
In the lozenge-shaped openings. Because
It is argued that these structures address themselves
To exclusively aesthetic concerns, like windmills
On a vast plain. To which it is answered
That there are no other questions than these,
Half squashed in mud, emerging out of the moment
We all live, learning to like it. No sonnet
On this furthest strip of land, no pebbles,

No plants. To extend one's life
All day on the dirty stone of some plaza,
Unaware among the pretty lunging of the wind,
Light and shade, is like coming out of
A coma that is a white, interesting country,
Prepared to lose the main memory in a meeting
By torchlight under the twisted end of the stairs.

THE WRONG KIND OF INSURANCE

I teach in a high school
And see the nurses in some of the hospitals,
And if all teachers are like that
Maybe I can give you a buzz some day,
Maybe we can get together for lunch or coffee or something.

The white marble statues in the auditorium
Are colder to the touch than the rain that falls
Past the post-office inscription about rain or snow
Or gloom of night. I think
About what these archaic meanings mean,
That unfurl like a rope ladder down through history,
To fall at our feet like crocuses.

All of our lives is a rebus
Of little wooden animals painted shy,
Terrific colors, magnificent and horrible,
Close together. The message is learned
The way light at the edge of a beach in autumn is learned.
The seasons are superimposed.
In New York we have winter in August
As they do in Argentina and Australia.
Spring is leafy and cold, autumn pale and dry.
And changes build up
Forever, like birds released into the light
Of an August sky, falling away forever
To define the handful of things we know for sure,
Followed by musical evenings.

Yes, friends, these clouds pulled along on invisible ropes
Are, as you have guessed, merely stage machinery,
And the funny thing is it knows we know
About it and still wants us to go on believing

In what it so unskillfully imitates, and wants
To be loved not for that but for itself:
The murky atmosphere of a park, tattered
Foliage, wise old treetrunks, rainbow tissue-paper wadded
Clouds down near where the perspective
Intersects the sunset, so we may know
We too are somehow impossible, formed of so many different things,
Too many to make sense to anybody.
We straggle on as quotients, hard-to-combine
Ingredients, and what continues
Does so with our participation and consent.

Try milk of tears, but it is not the same.
The dandelions will have to know why, and your comic
Dirge routine will be lost on the unfolding sheaves
Of the wind, a lucky one, though it will carry you
Too far, to some manageable, cold, open
Shore of sorrows you expected to reach,
Then leave behind.
                                        Thus, friend, this distilled,
Dispersed musk of moving around, the product
Of leaf after transparent leaf, of too many
Comings and goings, visitors at all hours.
                                                                  Each night
Is trifoliate, strange to the touch.

THE SERIOUS DOLL

The kinds of thing are more important than the
Individual thing, though the specific is supremely
Interesting. Right? As each particular
Goes over Niagara Falls in a barrel one may
Justifiably ask: Where does this come from?
Whither goes my concern? What you are wearing
Has vanished along with other concepts.
They are lined up by the factory balcony railing
Against blue sky with some clumsy white paper clouds
Pasted on it. Where does the east meet the west?
At sunset there is a choice of two smiles: discreet or serious.
In this best of all possible worlds, that is enough.

FRIENDS

I like to speak in rhymes,
because I am a rhyme myself.
NIJINSKY

I saw a cottage in the sky.
I saw a balloon made of lead.
I cannot restrain my tears, and they fall
On my left hand and on my silken tie,
But I cannot and do not want to hold them back.

One day the neighbors complain about an unpleasant odor
Coming from his room. *I went for a walk*
But met no friends. Another time I go outside
Into the world. It rocks on and on.
It was rocking before I saw it
And is presumably doing so still.

The banker lays his hand on mine.
His face is as clean as a white handkerchief.
We talk nonsense as usual.
I trace little circles on the light that comes in
Through the window on saw-horse legs.
Afterwards I see that we are three.
Someone had entered the room while I was discussing my
  money problems.
I wish God would put a stop to this. I
Turn and see the new moon through glass. I am yanked away
So fast I lose my breath, a not unpleasant feeling.

I feel as though I had been carrying the message for years
On my shoulders like Atlas, never feeling it
Because of never having known anything else. In another way
I am involved with the message. I want to put it down
(In two senses of "put it down") so that you
May understand the agreeable destiny that awaits us.
You sigh. Your sighs will admit of no impatience,

Only a vast crater lake, vast as the sea,
In which the sky, smaller than that, is reflected.

I reach for my hat
And am bound to repeat with tact
The formal greeting I am charged with.
No one makes mistakes. No one runs away
Any more. I bite my lip and
Turn to you. Maybe now you understand.

The feeling is a jewel like a pearl.

THE THIEF OF POETRY

To you
my friend who
was in this

street once
were on it
getting

in with it
getting on with it
though

only passing by
a smell of hamburgers
that day

an old mattress
and a box spring
as it

darkened
filling the empty
rumble

of a street
in decay of time
it fell out that

there was no
remaining
whether out of a wish

to be moving on
or frustrated
willingness to stay

here to stand
still
the moment

had other plans
and now in this
jungle of darkness

the future still makes plans
O ready to go
Conceive of your plight

more integrally
the snow
that day

buried all but the most obtuse
only the most generalized
survives

the low profile
becomes a constant again
the line of ocean

of shore
nestling
confident

impermanent
to rise again
in new

vicissitude
in explicit
triumph

drowns the hum
of space
the false point

of the stars
in specific
new way of happening

Now
no one remembers
the day you walked a certain distance

along the beach
and then
walked back

it seems
in your tracks
because it

was ending
for the first time
yes but now

is another way of
spreading out
toward the end

the linear style
is discarded
though this is

not realized for centuries
meanwhile
another way of living had come and gone

leaving its width
behind
now the tall cedars

had become locked into
the plan
so that everywhere

you looked
was burning
inferential

interior space
not for colonies
but already closed

turned in on itself
its back
as beautiful as the sea

where you go up
and say the word
eminence

to yourself
all was lived in
had been lived in

was coming to an end
again
in the featureless present

that was expanding to
cloister it
this just a little too

comic parable
and so insure the second
beginning

of that day seen against the street
of whichever way
you walked and talked

knowing not knowing
the thing that was describing you
and not knowing

your taller
well somehow more informed
bearing

as you wind down
only a second
it did matter

you come back so seldom
but it's all right
the way of staying

you started comes back
procession into the fire
into the sky

the dream you lost
firm in its day
reassured and remembered.

THE ICE-CREAM WARS

Although I mean it, and project the meaning
As hard as I can into its brushed-metal surface,
It cannot, in this deteriorating climate, pick up
Where I leave off. It sees the Japanese text
(About two men making love on a foam-rubber bed)
As among the most massive secretions of the human spirit.
Its part is in the shade, beyond the iron spikes of the fence,
Mixing red with blue. As the day wears on
Those who come to seem reasonable are shouted down
(*Why you old goat!* Look who's talkin'. Let's see you
Climb off that tower—the waterworks architecture, both stupid and
Grandly humorous at the same time, is a kind of mask for him,
Like a seal's face. Time and the weather
Don't always go hand in hand, as here: sometimes
One is slanted sideways, disappears for awhile.
Then later it's forget-me-not time, and rapturous
Clouds appear above the lawn, and the rose tells
The old old story, the pearl of the orient, occluded
And still apt to rise at times.)

A few black smudges
On the outer boulevards, like squashed midges
And the truth becomes a hole, something one has always known,
A heaviness in the trees, and no one can say
Where it comes from, or how long it will stay—

A randomness, a darkness of one's own.

VALENTINE

Like a serpent among roses, like an asp
Among withered thornapples I coil to
And at you. The name of the castle is you,
El Rey. It is an all-night truck-stop
Offering the best coffee and hamburgers in Utah.
It is most beautiful and nocturnal by daylight.
Seven layers: moss-agate, coral, aventurine,
Carnelian, Swiss lapis, obsidian—maybe others.
You know now that it has the form of a string
Quartet. The different parts are always meddling with each other,
Pestering each other, getting in each other's way
So as to withdraw skillfully at the end, leaving—what?
A new kind of emptiness, maybe bathed in freshness,
Maybe not. Maybe just a new kind of emptiness.

You are smart but the weather of this day startles and japes at you. You come out of it in pieces. Always pursuing you is the knowledge that I am there unable to turn around, unable to confront you with your otherness. This is another one of my houses, the one in Hampstead, the brick one in the middle of the block that you never saw though you passed along that street many times, sometimes in spring with a light drizzle blowing that made you avert your gaze, sometimes at the height of summer where the grandeur of the ideas of the trees swamped your ideas about everything, so you never saw my house. It was near where Arthur Rackham lived. I can't quite remember the name of the street—some partly legible inscription on a Victorian urn: E and then MEL (E?), perhaps a Latin exhortation to apples or heroism, and down in the dim part a name like "Rossiter," but that is too far down. Listen, I never meant for you not to be in my house. But you couldn't because you were it.

In this part I reflect on the difficulty and surprise of being you. It may never get written. Some things are simultaneously too boring and too exciting to write about. This has to be one of them. Some day, when we're stoned . . . Meanwhile, write to me. I enjoy and appreciate your phone calls, but it's nice to get cards and letters too—so keep 'em comin'!

Through bearded twilight I hear things like "Now see here, young man!" or "Henry Groggins, you old reprobate!" or "For an hour Lester has been staring at budget figures, making no progress." I know these things are, that they are. At night there are a few things, and they slide along to make room for others. Seen through an oval frame, one of the walls of a parlor. The wallpaper is a conventionalized pattern, the sliced okra and star-anise one, held together with crudely gummed links of different colored paper, among which purple predominates, stamped over a flocked background of grisaille shepherdesses and dogs urinating against fire hydrants. To reflect on the consummate skill with which the artist has rendered the drops as they bounce off the hydrant and collect in a gleaming sun-yellow pool below the curb is a sobering experience. Only the shelf of the mantelpiece shows. At each end, seated on pedestals turned slightly away from one another, two aristocratic bisque figures, a boy in delicate cerise and a girl in cornflower blue. Their shadows join in a grotesque silhouette. In the center, an ancient clock whose tick acts as the metronome for the sound of their high voices. Presently the mouths of the figures open and shut, after the mode of ordinary conversation.

Thought I'd
Row across to you this afternoon,
My Irina! Always writing your beloved articles,
I see. Happened on one only recently in one of the more progressive
journals.

Brilliantly written, or so it seemed, but isn't your thought a bit too
Advanced by present-day standards? Of course, there was much truth
In what you said, but don't you feel the public sometimes has more
truth
Than it can cope with? I don't mean that you should . . . well, "fib,"
But perhaps, well, heh heh, temper the wind to the shorn lamb
A bit. Eh? How about it, old boy?
Or are you so in love with your "advanced" thinking that
everything else
Seems old hat to you, including my conversation no doubt? In that
Case I ought to be getting on. Goodness, I've a four-thirty
appointment and it's
Already five after. What have you done with my hat?

These things I write for you and you only.
Do not judge them too harshly. Temper the wind,
As he was saying. They are infant things
That may grow up to be children, perhaps—who knows?—
Even adults some day, but now they exist only in the blindness
Of your love for me and are the proof of it.
You can't think about them too long
Without knocking them over. Your castle is a house of cards,
The old-fashioned kind of playing cards, towering farther
Than the eye can see into the clouds, and it is also built on
Shifting sands, its base slurps out of sight too. I am the inhabitable one.
But my back is as a door to you, now open, now shut,
And your kisses are as dreams, or an elixir
Of radium, or flowers of some kind.
Remember about what I told you.

BLUE SONATA

Long ago was the then beginning to seem like now
As now is but the setting out on a new but still
Undefined way. *That* now, the one once
Seen from far away, is our destiny
No matter what else may happen to us. It is
The present past of which our features,
Our opinions are made. We are half it and we
Care nothing about the rest of it. We
Can see far enough ahead for the rest of us to be
Implicit in the surroundings that twilight is.
We know that this part of the day comes every day
And we feel that, as it has its rights, so
We have our right to be ourselves in the measure
That we are in it and not some other day, or in
Some other place. The time suits us
Just as it fancies itself, but just so far
As we not give up that inch, breath
Of becoming before becoming may be seen,
Or come to seem all that it seems to mean now.

The things that were coming to be talked about
Have come and gone and are still remembered
As being recent. There is a grain of curiosity
At the base of some new thing, that unrolls
Its question mark like a new wave on the shore.
In coming to give, to give up what we had,
We have, we understand, gained or been gained
By what was passing through, bright with the sheen
Of things recently forgotten and revived.
Each image fits into place, with the calm
Of not having too many, of having just enough.
We live in the sigh of our present.

If that was all there was to have
We could re-imagine the other half, deducing it
From the shape of what is seen, thus
Being inserted into its idea of how we
Ought to proceed. It would be tragic to fit
Into the space created by our not having arrived yet,
To utter the speech that belongs there,
For progress occurs through re-inventing
These words from a dim recollection of them,
In violating that space in such a way as
To leave it intact. Yet we do after all
Belong here, and have moved a considerable
Distance; our passing is a façade.
But our understanding of it is justified.

SPRING LIGHT

The buildings, piled so casually
Behind each other, are "suggestions
Which, while only suggestions,
We hope you will take seriously." Off into
The blue. Getting there is easier,
But then we hope you will come down.
There is a great deal on the ground today,
Not just mud, but things of some importance,
Too. Like, silver paint. How do you feel
About it? And, is this a silver age?
Yeah. I suppose so. But I keep looking at the cigarette
Burns on the edge of the sink, left over
From last winter. Your argument's
Neatly beyond any paths I'm likely to take,
Here, or when I eventually leave here.

SYRINGA

Orpheus liked the glad personal quality
Of the things beneath the sky. Of course, Eurydice was a part
Of this. Then one day, everything changed. He rends
Rocks into fissures with lament. Gullies, hummocks
Can't withstand it. The sky shudders from one horizon
To the other, almost ready to give up wholeness.
Then Apollo quietly told him: "Leave it all on earth.
Your lute, what point? Why pick at a dull pavan few care to
Follow, except a few birds of dusty feather,
Not vivid performances of the past." But why not?
All other things must change too.
The seasons are no longer what they once were,
But it is the nature of things to be seen only once,
As they happen along, bumping into other things, getting along
Somehow. That's where Orpheus made his mistake.
Of course Eurydice vanished into the shade;
She would have even if he hadn't turned around.
No use standing there like a gray stone toga as the whole wheel
Of recorded history flashes past, struck dumb, unable to utter
an intelligent
Comment on the most thought-provoking element in its train.
Only love stays on the brain, and something these people,
These other ones, call life. Singing accurately
So that the notes mount straight up out of the well of
Dim noon and rival the tiny, sparkling yellow flowers
Growing around the brink of the quarry, encapsulates
The different weights of the things.

But it isn't enough
To just go on singing. Orpheus realized this
And didn't mind so much about his reward being in heaven
After the Bacchantes had torn him apart, driven
Half out of their minds by his music, what it was doing to them.
Some say it was for his treatment of Eurydice.

But probably the music had more to do with it, and
The way music passes, emblematic
Of life and how you cannot isolate a note of it
And say it is good or bad. You must
Wait till it's over. "The end crowns all,"
Meaning also that the "tableau"
Is wrong. For although memories, of a season, for example,
Melt into a single snapshot, one cannot guard, treasure
That stalled moment. It too is flowing, fleeting;
It is a picture of flowing, scenery, though living, mortal,
Over which an abstract action is laid out in blunt,
Harsh strokes. And to ask more than this
Is to become the tossing reeds of that slow,
Powerful stream, the trailing grasses
Playfully tugged at, but to participate in the action
No more than this. Then in the lowering gentian sky
Electric twitches are faintly apparent first, then burst forth
Into a shower of fixed, cream-colored flares. The horses
Have each seen a share of the truth, though each thinks,
"I'm a maverick. Nothing of this is happening to me,
Though I can understand the language of birds, and
The itinerary of the lights caught in the storm is fully apparent to me.
Their jousting ends in music much
As trees move more easily in the wind after a summer storm
And is happening in lacy shadows of shore-trees, now, day after day."

But how late to be regretting all this, even
Bearing in mind that regrets are always late, too late!
To which Orpheus, a bluish cloud with white contours,
Replies that these are of course not regrets at all,
Merely a careful, scholarly setting down of
Unquestioned facts, a record of pebbles along the way.
And no matter how all this disappeared,

Or got where it was going, it is no longer
Material for a poem. Its subject
Matters too much, and not enough, standing there helplessly
While the poem streaked by, its tail afire, a bad
Comet screaming hate and disaster, but so turned inward
That the meaning, good or other, can never
Become known. The singer thinks
Constructively, builds up his chant in progressive stages
Like a skyscraper, but at the last minute turns away.
The song is engulfed in an instant in blackness
Which must in turn flood the whole continent
With blackness, for it cannot see. The singer
Must then pass out of sight, not even relieved
Of the evil burthen of the words. Stellification
Is for the few, and comes about much later
When all record of these people and their lives
Has disappeared into libraries, onto microfilm.
A few are still interested in them. "But what about
So-and-so?" is still asked on occasion. But they lie
Frozen and out of touch until an arbitrary chorus
Speaks of a totally different incident with a similar name
In whose tale are hidden syllables
Of what happened so long before that
In some small town, one indifferent summer.

FANTASIA ON "THE NUT-BROWN MAID"

HE

Be it right or wrong, these men among
Others in the park, all those years in the cold,
Are a plain kind of thing: bands
Of acanthus and figpeckers. At
The afternoon closing you walk out
Of the dream crowding the walls and out
Of life or whatever filled up
Those days and seemed to be life.
You borrowed its colors, the drab ones
That are so popular now, though only
For a minute, and extracted a fashion
That wasn't really there. You are
Going, I from your thought rapidly
To the green wood go, alone, a banished man.

SHE

But now always from your plaint I
Relive, revive, springing up careless,
Dust geyser in city absentmindedness,
And all day it is writ and said:
We round women like corners. They are the friends
We are always saying goodbye to and then
Bumping into the next day. School has closed
Its doors on a few. Saddened, she rose up
And untwined the gears of that blank, blossoming day.
"So much for Paris, and the living in this world."
But I was going to say
It differently, about the way
Time is sorting us all out, keeping you and her
Together yet apart, in a give-and-take, push-pull

Kind of environment. And then, packed like sardines,
Our wit arises, survives automatically. We imbibe it.

HE

What was all the manner
Between them, let us discuss, the sponge
Of night pick us up with much else, carry
Some distance, so all the pain and fear
Will never be heard by anybody. Gasping
On your porch, but I look to new season
Which is exactly lost. "I am the knight,
I come by night." We will say all these
To the other, in turn. And now impatient for
Sleep will have strayed over the
Frontier to pass the time, and it might
As well, dried baby's breath stuck in an old
Bottle, and no man puts out to sea from these
Coves, secure or not, dwelling in persuasion.

SHE

It's as I thought: there there is
Nothing solid, nothing one can build on. The
Force may have ebbed in the green wood.
Here is nothing, not even
Lazy slipping away, feeling of being abandoned, a
Distant curl of smoke above a car
Graveyard. Instead, the shadows stand
Straight out. Uninvited, light grabs its due;
What is eaten away becomes etched impression
Of mutability, but nothing backs it up.
We may as well begin the litany here:

How all that forgotten past seasons us, prepares
Us for each other, now that the mathematics
Of winter is starting to point it out.

HE

It is true, a truer story.
Self-knowledge frosts each action, each step taken
Freely. Life is a living picture.
Alone, I can bind you like a pleated scarf
But beyond that is much that might be
Examined for the purpose of examining it.
The ends stream back in the wind, it is too dark
To see them but I can feel them.
As Naming-of-Cares you precede the objection
To each, implying a Land of Cockaigne
Syndrome. You get around this as though
The eternally revised geography of spring meant
Something beyond its own sense of exaltation,
And love were cause for self-congratulation.

SHE

I might hide somewhere. I want to fly but keep
My morality, motley as it is, just by
Encouraging these branching diversions around an axis.
So when suddenly a cloud blackens the whole
Day just before noon, this is merely
Timing. So even when darkness swings further
Back, it indicates, must indicate, an order,
Albeit a restricted one, which tends to prove that idle
Civilizations once existed under a loose heading like
"The living and the dead." To learn more

Isn't my way, and anyway the dark green
Ring around the basin postulates
More than the final chapter of this intriguing
Unfinished last chapter. It's in the public domain.

HE

But you will take comfort in it again.
Others, patient murderers, cultivated,
Sympathetic, in time will have subtly
Switched the background from parallel rain-lines
To the ambiguities of "the deep," and in
Doing so will have wheeled an equestrian statue up
Against the sky's façade, the eye of God, cantering
So as not to fall back nor yet trample the cold
Pourings of sunlight. You will have the look
Reflected on your face. The great squash domes seem
To vindicate us all, yet belong to no one.
Meanwhile others will grow up and fuck and
Get older, beating like weeds against the door,
But this wasn't anticipated. You caught them off guard.

SHE

What I hear scraping at the door
Is palaver of multitudes who decided to come back,
Having set out too soon, and something must be
Done about them, names must be written down,
Or simply by being hoarse one whole side
Of the world won't count any more,
The side with the story of our lives
And our relatives' on it, the memory
Of the day you bicycled over.

But the reason for the even, tawny flow
Of the morning as it turned was the thought of riding
Back down all those hills that were so hard
To get up, and climbing the ones you had
Coasted down before, like mirror-writing.

HE

And when the flourish under the signature,
A miniature beehive with a large bee on it, was
Finished, you chose a view of distant factories,
Tall smokestacks, anything. It didn't matter
So long as it was emptied of all but a drop
At the bottom like the medicine bottle that is thrown away.
The catch in the voice goes out of style then,
The period of civilities is long past.
Strange we should be continually waking up
To a barbaric calm that has probably
Always supported us, while still
Apologizing to the off-white walls we saw through
Years ago. But it stays this way.

SHE

What happened was you had finished
Nine-tenths of it before the great explosion,
The meteorite or whatever it was that tore out the
Huge crater eight miles in diameter.
Then somehow you spliced the bleeding wires,
Made it presentable long enough for
Inspection, then collapsed and slept until
The part where she takes the bus. And all
Because someone in a department store made some

Cryptic allusion, or so you thought as that person
Passed by, reducing the architecture of a life
To a minus quantity. There was no way
Back out of this because it wasn't a departure.

HE

I once stole a pencil, but now the list with my name on it
Disgusts me. It is the horizon, tilted like the deck
Of a ship. And beyond, what must be the real
Horizon congeals into a blue roebuck whose shadow
Hardens every upturned face it trails across
And sets a blister there. If there was still time
To turn back, you must not follow me, but rather
Stay in your living, in your time,
Sizing up the future as accurately as the woman
In the old photograph, and, like her, turn away,
Your hand barely grazing the top of the little doric column.
Anything outside what the sheaf of rays delineates
For the moment is pain and at least illusion,
A piece of not very good news.

SHE

Then we must be like each other, because this afternoon's
Ballast barely holds back the rising landscape
Of premonitions against that now distant (yet all too
Contemporaneous) magnesium flare in which
The habits of a moment, like wrinkles in a piece of backcloth,
Plummeted into the space under the stage
Through a trapdoor carelessly left open,
Joining other manifestations of human stick-to-itiveness
In a "semi-retirement" which has its own rewards

Except the solution only comes about much later, and then
Won't entirely fit all the clues of the atmosphere
(Books, dishes and bathrooms), but is
Empty and vigilant, but too late to make the train,
And at night stands like tall buildings, disembodied,
Vaporous, rhapsodic, going on and on about something
That happened in the past, at the point where the recent
Past ends and the darker one begins.

HE

But since "we know what we are, but know not
What we may be," and it's later now, the romance
Of moderation takes over again. Something has to be
Living, not everyone can afford the luxury of
Just being, not alive but being, at the center,
The perfumed, patterned center. Perhaps it's all fun
But we won't know till we see it, as on a windless day
It suddenly becomes obvious how wonderful the fields are
Before it all sickens and fades to a mélange
Of half-truths, this gray dump. Then double trouble
Arrives, Beppo and Zeppo confront one
Out of a hurricane of colored dots, twin
Windshield wipers dealing the accessories:
Woe, wrack, wet—probably another kingdom.

SHE

I was going to say that the sky
Could never become that totally self-absorbed, bachelor's-
Button blue, yet it has, and nothing is any safer for it,
Though the outlines of what we did stay just a second longer
On the etching of the forest, and we know enough not
To go there. If brimstone were the same as the truth
A gate deep in the ground would unlock to the fumbling

Of a certain key and the dogs at the dog races
Would circumambulate each in his allotted groove
Casting an exaggeratedly long shadow, while other
Malcontents, troublemakers, *esprits frondeurs* moved up
To dissolve in the brightness of the footlights. I would
Withstand, bow in hand, to grieve them. So it is time
To wake up, to commingle with the little walking presences, all
Somehow related, to each other and through each other to us,
Characters in the opera *The Flood*, by the great anonymous composer.

HE

Mostly they are
Shoals, even tricks of the light, armies
In debacle, helter skelter, pell mell,
Fleeing us who sometime did us seek,
And there is no place, nothing
To hide in, if it took weeks and months
With time running out. Nothing could be done.
Those ramparts, granular as Saturn's rings,
That seem some tomb of pleasures, a Sans Souci,
Are absent clouds. The real diversions on the ground
Are shrub and nettle, planing the way
For asking me to come down, and the snow, the frost, the rain,
The cold, the heat, for dry or wet
We must lodge on the plain. . . . Later, dying
"Of complications," only it must really have been much later, her hair
Had that whited look. Now it's darker.

SHE

And an intruder is present.
But it always winds down like this
To the rut of night. Boats no longer come
Plying along the sides of docks in this part

Of the world. We are alone. Only by climbing
A low bluff does the intent get filled in
Along the edge, and then only subtly.
Evening weaves along these open tracts almost
Until the solemn tolling of a bell
Launches its moment of pain and obscurity, wider
Than any net can seize, or star presage. Further on it says
That all the missing parts must be tracked down
By coal-light or igloo-light because
In so doing we navigate these our passages,
And take sides on certain issues, are
Emphatically pro or con about what concerns us,
Such as the strangeness of our architecture,
The diffuse quality of our literature.

HE

Or does each tense fit, and each desire
Drown in the lake of one vague one, featureless
And indeterminate? Which is why one's own wish
Keeps getting granted for someone else? In the forest
Are no clean sheets, no other house
But leaves and boughs. How many
Other things can one want? Nice hair
And eyes, galoshes on a rainy day? For those who go
Under the green helm know it lets itself
Become known, at different moments, under different aspects.

SHE

Unless some movie did it first, or
A stranger came to the door and then the change
Was real until it went away. Or is it
Like a landscape in its inner folds, relaxed

And with the sense of there being about to be some more
Until the first part is digested and then it twists
Only because this is the way we can see things?
It is revisionism in that you are
Always trying to put some part of the past back in,
And although it fits it doesn't belong in the
Dark blue glass ocean of having been remembered again.
From earliest times we were cautioned not to get excited
About things, so this quality shows up so far only in
Slightly deeper tree-shadows that anticipate this PACING THE FLOOR
That takes in the walls, the window and the woods.

HE

Then it was as if a kind of embarrassment,
The product of a discretion lodged far back in the past,
Blotted them against a wall of haze.
Pursuing time this way, as a dog nudges a bone,
You find it has doubled back the flanges
Of night having now replaced the big daffy gray clouds.
O now no longer speak, but rather seem
In the way of gardens long ago turned away from,
And now no one any more will have to believe anything
He or she doesn't want to as golden light wholly
Saturates a wooden fence and speaks for everybody
In a native accent that sounds new and foreign.
But the hesitation stayed on, and came to be permanent
Because they were thinking about each other.

SHE

That's an unusual . . . as though a new crescent
Reached out and lapped at a succession of multitudes,
Diminished now, but still lively and true.
It seems to say: there are lots of differences inside.

There were differences when only you knew them.
Now they are an element, not themselves,
And hands are idle, or weigh the head
Like an outsize grapefruit, or an ocarina
Closes today with a comical wail.
Go in to them, see
What the session was about, how much they destroyed
And what preserved of what was meant to shuffle
Along in its time: hunched red shoulders
Of huntsmen, what they were doing
There in the grass, ribbons of time fluttering
From the four corners of a square masonry tower.

HE

Having draped ourselves in villas, across verandas
For so many years, having sampled
Rose petals and newspapers, we know that the eye of the storm,
As it moves majestically to engulf us, is alive
With the spirit of confusion, and that these birds
Are stamped with the same dream of exaltation moving
Toward the end. 'Tis said of old, soon
Hot, soon cold. There are other kinds of privacy
Coming in now, and soon,
In three or four months, enough leisure
To examine the claim of each
And to reward each according to his claim
On a sliding scale coinciding with the rush
Into later blue sun-divided weather.

SHE

No, but I dug these out of bureau drawers for you,
Told you which ones meant a lot to me,

Which ones I was frankly dubious about, and
Which were destined to blow away.
Who are we to suffer after this?
The fragrant cunt, the stubborn penis, winding
Paths of despair and memory, reproach in
The stairwell, and new confidence: "We'll
Do something about that," until a later date
When pines march stiffly right down to the edge of the water.
And after all this, finding
Someone at home, as though memory
Had placed chairs around
So that these seem to come and go in the present
And will escape the anger of a fixed
Destiny causing them to lean all the way over to one side
Like wind-heaped foam.

HE

It's enough that they are had,
Allowed to run loose.
As I was walking all alane
The idea of a field of particulars—that
Each is shaped, illustratable, accountable
To us and to no man—leached into the pervading
Gray-blue sense of moving somewhere with coevals,
Palmers and pardoners, a raucous yet erasable
Rout pent in the glimmer of
An American Bar. Whereupon Barry Sullivan-type avers
To Bruce Bennett-type that inert wet blackness is
Superior to boudoir light in which
Dull separateness blazes and is shriven and
Knows it isn't right.

SHE

And shall, like a Moebius strip
Of a tapestry, play to our absences and soothe them,
Whether in some deprived tropic or some
Boudoir-cave where it finds that just
Paying the interest on the bonanza is dressier.
Alas, but there are others, he thought, and we are children
Again, the children our parents were, trampling
Under foot the delicate boundary, last thing of day
Before night, that resurrects and comforts us here. Patience
Of articulation between us is still what it is,
No more and no less, but this time the night shift
Will have to be disturbed, and wiping out the quality
Of yesterday with the sponge of dreams is being phased out.

HE

You're making a big mistake. Just because Goofus has been lucky for you, you imagine others will make a fuss over you, all the others, who will matriculate. You'll be left with a trowel and a lot of empty flowerpots, imagining that the sun as it enters this window is somehow a blessing that will make up for everything else—those very years in the cold. That the running faucet is a sacred stream. That the glint of light from a silver ball on that far-off flagpole is the equivalent of a career devoted to life, to improving the minds and the welfare of others, when in reality it is a common thing like these, and less profitable than any hobby or sideline that is a source of retirement income, such as an antique stall, pecan harvest or root-beer stand. In short, although the broad outlines of your intentions are a credit to you, what fills them up isn't. You are like someone whose face was photographed in a crowd scene once and then gradually retreated from people's memories, and from life as well.

SHE

But the real "world"
Stretches its pretending into the side yard
Where I was waiting, at peace with my feelings, though now,
I see, resentful from the beginning for the change to happen
Like lilacs. We were walking
All along toward a door that seemed to recede
In the distance and now is somehow behind us, shut,
Though apparently it didn't lock automatically. How
Wonderful the fields are. They are
Like love poetry, all the automatic breathing going on
All around, and there are enchanted, many-colored
Things like houses to explore, if there were time,
But the house is built under a waterfall. The slanting
Roof and the walls are made of opaque glass, and
The emerald-green wall-to-wall carpeting is sopping moss.

HE

And last, perhaps, as darkness
Begins to infuse the lawns and silent streets
And the remote estuary, and thickens here, you mention
The slamming of a door I wasn't supposed to know about,
That took years. Each of us circles
Around some simple but vital missing piece of information,
And, at the end, as now, finding no substitute,
Writes his own mark grotesquely with a stick in snow,
The signature of many connected seconds of indecision.
What I am writing to say is, the timing, not
The contents, is what matters. All this could have happened
Long ago, or at least on some other day,
And not meant much except insofar as the eye

Extracts a progress from almost anything. But then
It wouldn't have become a toy.
And all the myths,
Legends and misinterpretations, would have scattered
At a single pistol shot. And it would no longer know what I know.

SHE

It was arriving now, the eyes thick
With their black music, the wooden misquotable side
Thrust forward. Tell about the affair she'd had
With Bennett Palmer, the Minnesota highwayman,
Back when she was staying at Lake Geneva, Wisc.,
In the early forties. That paynim'd
Go to any lengths to shut her up, now,
Now that the time of truth telling from tall towers
Had come. Only old Thomas à Tattamus with his two tups
Seemed really to care. Even Ellen herself
Could muster but a few weak saws about loving—how it leaves us
Naked at a time when we would rather be clothed, and
She looked all around the room with a satisfied air.
Everything was in order, even unto bareness, waiting to receive
Whatever stamp or seal. The light coming in off the kale
In the kaleyard outside was like the joyous, ravening
Light over the ocean the morning after a storm.
It hadn't betrayed her and it never would.

HE

To him, the holiday-making crowds were
Engines of a parallel disaster, the fulfilling
Of all prophecies between now and the day of
Judgment. Spiralling like fish,

Toward a distant, unperceived surface, was all
The reflection there was. Somewhere it had its opaque
Momentary existence.

But if each act

Is reflexive, concerned with itself on another level
As well as with us, the strangers who live here,
Can one advance one step further without sinking equally
Far back into the past? There was always something to see,
Something going on, for the historical past owed it
To itself, our historical present. Another month a huge
Used-car sale on the lawn shredded the sense of much
Of the sun coming through the wires, or a cape
Would be rounded by a slim white sail almost
Invisible in the specific design, or children would come
Clattering down fire escapes until the margin
Exploded into an ear of sky. Today the hospitals
Are light, airy places, tented clouds, and the weeping
In corridors is like autumn showers. It's beginning.

*

Unless this is the shelf of whatever happens? The cold sunrise attacks one side of the giant capital letters, bestirs a little the landmass as it sinks, grateful but asleep. And you too are a rebus from another century, your fiction in piles like lace, in that a new way of appreciating has been invented, that tomorrow will be quantitatively and qualitatively different—young love, cheerful, insubstantial things—and that these notions have been paraded before, though never with the flashing density climbing higher with you on the beanstalk until the jewelled mosaic of hills, ploughed fields and rivers agreed to be so studied and fell away forever, a gash of laughter, a sneeze of gold dust into the prism that weeps and remains solid.

Well had she represented the patient's history to his apathetic scrutiny. Always there was something to see, something going on, *for the historical past owed it to itself, our historical present.* There were visiting firemen, rumors of chattels on a spree, old men made up to look like young women in the polygon of night from which light sometimes breaks, to be sucked back, armies of foreigners who could not understand each other, the sickening hush just before the bleachers collapse, the inevitable uninvited and only guest who writes on the wall: I choose not to believe. It became a part of oral history. Things overheard in cafés assumed an importance previously reserved for letters from the front. The past was a dream of doctors and drugs. This wasn't misspent time. Oh, sometimes it'd seem like doing the same thing over and over, until I had passed beyond whatever the sense of it had been. Besides, hadn't it all ended a long time back, on some clear, washed-out afternoon, with a stiff breeze that seemed to shout: go back! For the moated past lives by these dreams of decorum that take into account any wisecracks made at their expense. It is not called living in a past. If history were only minding one's business, but, once under the gray shade of mist drawn across us . . . And who am I to speak this way, into a shoe? I know that evening is busy with lights, cars . . . That the curve will include me if I must stand here. My warm regards are cold, falling back to the vase again like a fountain. Responsible to whom? I have chosen this environment and it is handsome: a festive ruching of bare twigs against the sky, masks under the balconies

that

I sing alway

SHADOW TRAIN

THE PURSUIT OF HAPPINESS

It came about that there was no way of passing
Between the twin partitions that presented
A unified façade, that of a suburban shopping mall
In April. One turned, as one does, to other interests

Such as the tides in the Bay of Fundy. Meanwhile there was one
Who all unseen came creeping at this scale of visions
Like the gigantic specter of a cat towering over tiny mice
About to adjourn the town meeting due to the shadow,

An incisive shadow, too perfect in its outrageous
Regularity to be called to stand trial again,
That every blistered tongue welcomed as the first
Drops scattered by the west wind, and yet, knowing

That it would always ever afterwards be this way
Caused the eyes to faint, the ears to ignore warnings.
We knew how to get by on what comes along, but the idea
Warning, waiting there like a forest, not emptied, beckons.

PUNISHING THE MYTH

At first it came easily, with the knowledge of the shadow line
Picking its way through various landscapes before coming
To stand far from you, to bless you incidentally
In sorting out what was best for it, and most suitable,

Like snow having second thoughts and coming back
To be wary about this, to embellish that, as though life were a party
At which work got done. So we wiggled in our separate positions
And stayed in them for a time. After something has passed

You begin to see yourself as you would look to yourself on a stage,
Appearing to someone. But to whom? Ah, that's just it,
To have the manners, and the look that comes from having a secret
Isn't enough. But that "not enough" isn't to be worn like a livery,

To be briefly noticed, yet among whom should it be seen? I haven't
Thought about these things in years; that's my luck.
In time even the rocks will grow. And if you have curled and dandled
Your innocence once too often, what attitude isn't then really yours?

PARADOXES AND OXYMORONS

This poem is concerned with language on a very plain level.
Look at it talking to you. You look out a window
Or pretend to fidget. You have it but you don't have it.
You miss it, it misses you. You miss each other.

The poem is sad because it wants to be yours, and cannot.
What's a plain level? It is that and other things,
Bringing a system of them into play. Play?
Well, actually, yes, but I consider play to be

A deeper outside thing, a dreamed role-pattern,
As in the division of grace these long August days
Without proof. Open-ended. And before you know
It gets lost in the steam and chatter of typewriters.

It has been played once more. I think you exist only
To tease me into doing it, on your level, and then you aren't
there
Or have adopted a different attitude. And the poem
Has set me softly down beside you. The poem is you.

ANOTHER CHAIN LETTER

He had had it told to him on the sward
Where the fat men bowl, and told so that no one—
He least of all—might be sure in the days to come
Of the *exact* terms. Then, each turned back

To his business, as is customary on such occasions.
Months and months went by. The green squirearchy
Of the dandelions was falling through the hoop again
And no one, it seemed, had had the presence of mind

To initiate proceedings or stop the wheel
From the number it was backing away from as it stopped:
It was performing prettily; the puncture stayed unseen;
The wilderness seemed to like the eclogue about it

You wrote and performed, but really no one now
Saw any good in the cause, or any guilt. It was a conspiracy
Of right-handed notions. Which is how we all
Became partners in the pastoral doffing, the night we now knew.

THE IVORY TOWER

Another season, proposing a name and a distant resolution.
And, like the wind, all attention. Those thirsting ears,
Climbers on what rickety heights, have swept you
All alone into their confession, for it is as alone

Each of us stands and surveys this empty cell of time. Well,
What is there to do? And so a mysterious creeping motion
Quickens its demonic profile, bringing tears, to these eyes at least,
Tears of excitement. When was the last time you *knew* that?

Yet in the textbooks thereof you keep getting mired
In a backward innocence, although that too is something
That must be owned, together with the rest.
There is always some impurity. Help it along! Make room for it!

So that in the annals of this year be nothing but what is sobering:
A porch built on pilings, far out over the sand. Then it doesn't
Matter that the deaths come in the wrong order. All has been so
  easily
Written about. And you find the right order after all: play, the
  streets, shopping, time flying.

EVERY EVENING WHEN THE SUN GOES DOWN

The helmeted head is tilted up at you again
Through a question. Booze and pills?
Probably it has no cachet or real status
Beyond the spokes of the web of good intentions

That radiate a certain distance out from the crater, that is the smile,
That began it? Do you see yourself
Covered by this uniform of half regrets and
Inadmissible satisfactions, dazzling as the shower

Sucked back up into the peacock's-feather eye in the sky
As though through a straw, to connect up with your brain,
The thing given you tonight to wrestle with like an angel
Until dawn? The snuffer says it better. The cone

Squelches the wick, the insulted smoke jerks ceilingward
In the long time since we have been afraid, while the host
Is looking for ice cubes and a glass, is gone
Into the similarity of firmaments. "One last question."

THE FREEDOM OF THE HOUSE

A few more might have survived the fall
To read the afternoon away, navigating
In sullen peace, a finger at the lips,
From the beginning of one surf point to the end,

And again, and may have wondered why being alone
Is the condition of happiness, the substance
Of the golden hints, articulation in the hall outside,
And the condition as well of using that knowledge

To pleasure, always in confinement? Otherwise it fades
Like the rejoicing at the beginning of an opera, since we know
The seriousness of what lies ahead: that we can split open
The ripe exchanges, kisses, sighs, only in unholy

Solitude, and sample them here. It means that a disguised fate
Is weaving a net of heat lightning on the horizon, and that this
Will be neither bad nor good when experienced. Meanwhile
The night has been pushed back again, but cannot say where
it has been.

A PACT WITH SULLEN DEATH

Clearly the song will have to wait
Until the time when everything is serious.
Martyrs of fixed eye, with a special sigh,
Set down their goads. The skies have endured

Too long to be blasted into perdition this way,
And they fall, awash with blood and flowers.
In the dream next door they are still changing,
And the wakening changes too, into life.

"Is this life?" Yes, the last minute was too—
And the joy of informing takes over
Like the crackle of artillery fire in the outer suburbs
And I was going to wish that you too were the "I"

In the novel told in the first person that
This breathy waiting is, that we could crash through
The sobbing underbrush to the laughter that is under the ground,
Since anyone can wait. We have only to begin on time.

WHITE-COLLAR CRIME

Now that you've done it, say OK, that's it for a while.
His fault wasn't great; it was over-eagerness; it didn't deserve
The death penalty, but it's different when it happens
In your neighborhood, on your doorstep; the dropping light
spoilt nicely his

Name tags and leggings; all those things that belonged to him,
As it were, were thrown out overnight, onto the street.
So much for fashion. The moon decrees
That it be with us awhile to enhance the atmosphere

But in the long run serious concerns prevail, such as
What time is it and what are you going to do about that?
Gaily inventing brand names, place-names, you were surrounded
By such abundance, yet it seems only fair to start taking in

The washing now. *There was a boy.* Yet by the time the program
Is over, it turns out there was enough time and more than
enough things
For everybody to latch on to, and that in essence it's there, the
Young people and their sweet names falling, almost too many
of these.

AT THE INN

It was me here. Though. And whether this
Be rebus or me now, the way the grass is planted—
Red stretching far out to the horizon—
Surely prevails now. I shall return in the dark and be seen,

Be led to my own room by well-intentioned hands,
Placed in a box with a lid whose underside is dark
So as to grow, and shall grow
Taller than plumes out on the ocean,

Grazing historically. And shall see
The end of much learning, and other things
Out of control and it ends too soon, before hanging up.
So, laying his cheek against the dresser's wooden one,

He died making up stories, the ones
Not every child wanted to listen to.
And for a while it seemed that the road back
Was a track bombarded by stubble like a snow.

THE ABSENCE OF A NOBLE PRESENCE

If it was treason it was so well handled that it
Became unimaginable. No, it was ambrosia
In the alley under the stars and not this undiagnosable
Turning, a shadow in the plant of all things

That makes us aware of certain moments,
That the end is not far off since it will occur
In the present and this is the present.
No it was something not very subtle then and yet again

You've got to remember we don't see that much.
We see a portion of eaves dripping in the pastel book
And are aware that everything doesn't count equally—
There is dreaminess and infection in the sum

And since this too is of our everydays
It matters only to the one you are next to
This time, giving you a ride to the station.
It foretells itself, not the hiccup you both notice.

THE PROPHET BIRD

Then take the quicklime to the little tree.
And ask. So all will remain in place, percolating.
You see the sandlots still foaming with the blood of light
Though the source has been withdrawn.

What stunted fig or quince pierced those
Now empty pairs of parentheses. You shout
With the holy feeling of an oppressor, a scourge,
In order for the details to stick,

Like little blades of grass, stubborn and sick.
It is still too many ideas for a landscape.
In another time the tide would have turned, automobiles and
  the factory
Gushing in to frame the shining, clever, puzzled faces.

There would be even less to pick over, to glean.
But take this idea with you, please. It's all there,
Wrapped up. In the time it takes for nothing to happen
The places, the chairs and tables, the branches, were yours then.

QUALM

Warren G. Harding invented the word "normalcy,"
And the lesser-known "bloviate," meaning, one imagines,
To spout, to spew aimless verbiage. He never wanted to be president.
The "Ohio Gang" made him. He died in the Palace

Hotel in San Francisco, coming back from Alaska,
As his wife was reading to him, about him,
From *The Saturday Evening Post*. Poor Warren. He wasn't a bad egg,
Just weak. He loved women and Ohio.

This protected summer of high, white clouds, a new golf star
Flashes like confetti across the intoxicating early part
Of summer, almost to the end of August. The crowd is hysterical:
Fickle as always, they follow him to the edge

Of the inferno. But the fall is, deliciously, only his.
They shall communicate this and that and compute
Fixed names like "doorstep in the wind." The agony is permanent
Rather than eternal. He'd have noticed it. Poor Warren.

"Not spoiling it for later, yet few are
So febrile, so flourishing, and I extract
Digits from the Carolinas to fill out those days in Maine,
Only now trusting myself, as in the latter period I had not yet
learned to do."

And on top of all this one must still learn to judge the quality
Of those moments when it becomes necessary to break the rule,
To relax standards, bring light and chaos
Into the order of the house. A slatternly welcome

Suits some as well, no doubt, but the point is
There are still others whom we know nothing about
And who are growing, it seems, at a rate far in excess
Of the legislated norm, for whom the "psychological consequences"

Of the forest primeval of our inconsistency, nay, our lives
If you prefer, and you can quote me, could be "numbing."
Thus, one always reins in, after too much thoughtfulness, the joke
Prescription. Games were made to seem like that: the raw fruit,
bleeding.

OH, NOTHING

The tent stitch is repeated in the blue and red
Letters on the blocks. Love is spelled L-O-V-E
And is echoed farther down by fear. These two are sisters
But the youngest and most beautiful sister

Is called Forward Animation. It all makes sense
If you look at her through the clock. Now,
Such towns and benign legends as were distilled
To produce this moment of silence are dissolved

In the stream of history. Of her it may be said
That what she says, she knows, and it will always come undone
Around her, as you are thinking, and so the choice
Is still and always yours, and yet

You may move on, untouched. The glassy,
Chill surface of the cascade reflected her,
Her opinions and future, de-defining you. To be amused this way
Is to be immortal, as water gushes down the sides of the globe.

OF THE ISLANDS

Then the thirty-three-year-old man
Then the young but no longer powerfully young man
Gnashed at the towel's edge   chewed the rag
Brought it home to him right out   sighed with the force of

Palm winds: to do it unto others
Is to leave many undone   and the carvings that are "quite cute"
May end up as yours   dry in your storehouse
And this should be good for you yet

"Not as a gift but as a sign of transition"
The way all things spread and seem to remain under the lolling
Fronds and it is not your way as yet.
Only to be an absentee frees from the want of speculation

Drawing out conversations in the lobby   more than you care
And each gift returns home to the bearer   idly, at suppertime
Odd that he noticed you   diminished in this case, but with any
The true respect conserves   the hoofprint in the dust.

FARM FILM

Takeitapart, no one understands how you can just do
This to yourself. Balancing a long pole on your chin
And seeing only the ooze of foliage and blue sunlight
Above. At the same time you have not forgotten

The attendant itch, but, being occupied solely with making
Ends meet, or the end, believe that it will live, raised
In secrecy, into an important yet invisible destiny, unfulfilled.
If the dappled cows and noon plums ever thought of

Answering you, your answer would be like the sun, convinced
It knows best, maybe having forgotten someday. But for this
She looked long for one clothespin in the grass, the rime
And fire of midnight etched each other out, into importance

That is like a screen sometimes. So many
Patterns to choose from, they the colliding of all dispirited
Illustration on our lives, that will rise in its time like
Temperature, and mean us, and then faint away.

HERE EVERYTHING IS STILL FLOATING

But, it's because the liquor of summer nights
Accumulates in the bottom of the bottle.
Suspenders brought it to its, this, level, not
The tempest in a teapot of a private asylum, laughter on the
back steps,

Not mine, in fine; I must concentrate on how disappointing
It all has to be while rejoicing in my singular
Un-wholeness that keeps it an event to me. These, these young guys
Taking a shower with the truth, living off the interest of their

Sublime receptivity to anything, can disentangle the whole
Lining of fabricating living from the instantaneous
Pocket it explodes in, enters the limelight of history from,
To be gilded and regilded, waning as its legend waxes,

Disproportionate and triumphant. Still I enjoy
The long sweetness of the simultaneity, yours and mine,
ours and mine,
The mosquitoey summer night light. Now about your poem
Called this poem: it stays and must outshine its welcome.

JOE LEVIATHAN

Just because I wear a voluminous cap
With a wool-covered wooden button at its peak, the cries of children
Are upon me, passing through me. The season at this time
Offers no other spectacle for the curious part-time executioner.

In his house they speak of rope. They skate past the window.
I have seen and know
Bad endings lumped with the good. They are in the future.
And therefore cannot be far off.

The bank here is quite steep
And casts its shadow over the river floor.
An exploration, a field trip, might be worth making.
We could have made some nice excursions together.

Then he took a bat and the clams and
Where hope is the door it is stained with the strong stench of brine.
Inside too. The window frames have been removed. I mean
He can pass with me in the meaning and we still not see ourselves.

SOME OLD TIRES

This was mine, and I let it slip through my fingers.
Nevertheless, I do not want, in this airy and pleasant city,
To be held back by valors that were mine
Only for the space of a dream instant, before continuing

To be someone else's. Because there's too much to
Be done that doesn't fit, and the parts that get lost
Are the reasonable ones just because they got lost
And were forced to suffer transfiguration by finding their way home

To a forgotten spot way out in the fields. To have always
Had the wind for a friend is no recommendation. Yet some
Disagree, while still others claim that signs of fatigue
And mended places are, these offshore days, open

And a symbol of what must continue
After the ring is closed on us. The furniture,
Taken out and examined under the starlight, pleads
No contest. And the backs of those who sat there before.

A PRISON ALL THE SAME

Spoken over a yellow kitchen table (just the ticket
For these recycling-minded times): *You've got to show them who you are.*
Just being a person doesn't work anymore. Many of them drink beer.
A crisis or catastrophe goes off in their lives

Every few hours. They don't get used to it, having no memory.
Nor do they think it's better that way. What happens for them
Is part of them, an appendage. There's no room to step back
To get a perspective. The old one shops and thinks. The fragrant bulbs

In the cellar are no use either. Last week a man was here.
But just try sorting it out when you're on top
Of your destiny, like angels elbowing each other on the head of a pin.
Not until someone falls, or hesitates, does the renewal occur,

And then it's only for a second, like a breath of air
On a hot, muggy afternoon with no air conditioning. I was scared
Then. Now it's over. It can be removed like a sock
And mended, a little. One for the books.

DRUNKEN AMERICANS

I saw the reflection in the mirror
And it doesn't count, or not enough
To make a difference, fabricating itself
Out of the old, average light of a college town,

And afterwards, when the bus trip
Had depleted my pocket of its few pennies
He was seen arguing behind steamed glass,
With an invisible proprietor. What if you can't own

This one either? For it seems that all
Moments are like this: thin, unsatisfactory
As gruel, worn away more each time you return to them.
Until one day you rip the canvas from its frame

And take it home with you. You think the god-given
Assertiveness in you has triumphed
Over the stingy scenario: these objects are real as meat,
As tears. We are all soiled with this desire, at the last moment,
 the last.

SOMETHING SIMILAR

I, the city mouse, have traveled from a long ways away
To be with you with my news. Now you have my passport
With its color photo on it, to be sweet with you
As the times allow. I didn't say that because it's true,

I said it from a dim upstairs porch into the veiled
Shapely masses of this country you are the geography of
So you can put it in your wallet. That's all we can do
For the time being. Elegance has been halted for the duration

And may not be resumed again. The bare hulk tells us
Something, but mostly about what a strain it was to be brought
To such a pass, and then abandoned. So we may never
Again feel fully confident of the stratagem that bore us

And lived on a certain time after that. And it went away
Little by little, as most things do. To profit
By this mainstream is today's chore and adventure. He
Who touches base first at dusk is possessed first, then wins.

PENNY PARKER'S MISTAKE

That it could not be seen as constituting an endorsement
Any way she looked, up, down, around, around again,
  always the same
For her, always her now, was in the way it winked back.
For naturally, to be selling these old Indian dinosaur

Eggs and to be in some obscure way in their debt, not
For the modest living they provided, rather in having come to know
Them at all (not everybody need know everybody, and when you
Stop to think of it, this fits each of us tighter than

Any of the others) was the throwback to the earlier
Age each dreamed, a dream with little gold flecks
And reflection of wet avenues in the japanned facing of it.
Now, naturally we caring for the success of the success

Cannot cancel postures from some earlier decade of this century
That come to invade our walking like the spokes of an umbrella
And in some real way undermine the heaven of attitudes our
  chance was.
To be uncoiling this way, now, is the truer, but slier, stage of
  inebriation.

OR IN MY THROAT

To the poet as a basement quilt, but perhaps
To some reader a latticework of regrets, through which
You can see the funny street, with the ends of cars and the dust,
The thing we always forget to put in. For him

The two ends were the same except that he was in one
Looking at the other, and all his grief stemmed from that:
There was no way of appreciating anything else, how polite
People were for instance, and the dream, reversed, became

A swift nightmare of starlight on frozen puddles in some
Dread waste. Yet you always hear
How they are coming along. Someone always has a letter
From one of them, asking to be remembered to the boys, and all.

That's why I quit and took up writing poetry instead.
It's clean, it's relaxing, it doesn't squirt juice all over
Something you were certain of a minute ago and now your own face
Is a stranger and no one can tell you it's true. Hey, stupid!

UNTILTED

How tall the buildings were as I began
To live, and how high the rain that battered them!
Why, coming down them, as I often did at night,
Was a dream even before you reached the first gullies

And gave yourself over to thoughts of your own welfare.
It was the tilt of the wine in the cavalier's tilted glass
That documents so unerringly the faces and the mood in the room.
One slip would not be fatal, but then this is not a win or lose

Situation, so involved with living in the past on the ridge
Of the present, hearing its bells, breathing in its steam. . . .
And the shuttle never falters, but to draw an encouraging conclusion
From this would be considerable, too odd. Why not just

Breathe in with the courage of each day, recognizing yourself as one
Who must with difficulty get down from high places? Forget
The tourists—other people must travel too. It hurts now,
Cradled in the bend of your arm, the pure tear, doesn't it?

AT LOTUS LODGE

After her cat went away she led a quiet but remarkable
Existence. No tandem ways, but once out of town
The boxcars alternated with scenes of the religious life
In strong, faded colors. There is something in every room

Of the house, and in the powder room one truly inconceivable thing
That doesn't matter and is your name. You arrived late last night.
In between then and now is a circle for sleeping in
And we are right, at such moments, not to worry about the demands
of others;

They are like trees planted on a slope, too preoccupied
With the space dividing them to notice this singular tale of the past
And the thousand stories just like it, until one spills over
Into dreams, and they can point to it and say, "That's a dream,"

And go about their business. There is no compelling reason
For this moment to insist, yet it does, and has been with us
Down from the time England and Scotland were separate monarchies.
She got
No reply for your question, but that's understandable. All she had to
do was lie.

CORKY'S CAR KEYS

Despite, or because
Of its rambunctiousness, Kevin and Tracy—only appearances
Matter much—lingered in the not-night, red-painted brick
  background
Of festivals. And trees, old

Trees, like that one—sweet white dreams
Contain them, "in and out the windows."
Are the sunsets faster, now in old age, now
That you are inundated with them, or with something

To know me better? Yet despite, or because of, that, we have
To live here, so we should fix
This place up. A long time ago, in some earlier revival,
It seemed one of many handsome, felicitous choices—

How quickly the years pass. How could we tell the sound
Of the city at night would grow up too? And in its uncomfortable
Maturity dictate pyramids, process orders? Yet we can regulate
Everything in a little while, if he is truly the steeple.

NIGHT LIFE

I thought it was you but I couldn't tell.
It's so hard, working with people, you want them all
To like you and be happy, but they get in the way
Of their own predilections, it's like a stone

Blocking the mouth of a cave. And when you say, come on let's
Be individuals reveling in our separateness, yet twined
Together at the top by our hair, like branches, then it's OK
To go down into the garden at night and smoke cigarettes,

Except that nothing cares about the obstacles, the gravity
You had to overcome to reach this admittedly unimpressive
Stage in the chain of delusions leading to your freedom,
Or is that just one more delusion? Yet I like the way

Your hair is cropped, it's important, the husky fragrance
Breaking out of your voice, when I've talked too long
On the phone, addressing the traffic from my balcony
Again, launched far out over the thin ice once it begins to smile.

WRITTEN IN THE DARK

Telling it five, six, seven times a day,
Telling it like a bedtime story no one knows,
Telling it like a fortune, that happened a short time ago,
Like yesterday afternoon, so recently that it seems not to have

Quite happened yet. . . . All these and more were ways
Our love assumed to look like a state religion,
Like political wisdom. It's too bad that the two hands
Clenched between us fail us in their concreteness,

That we need some slogan to transform it all into autumn
Banners streaming, into flutter of bronze oak leaves, a surface
As intense and inquisitive as that of the sea. We stayed home.
We drank table wine, yellow then violet, wormwood color,

Color of the sound of waves sweeping across a flat beach
Farther than ever before, taking greater liberties in the name
Of liberty. But it shouldn't. Don't you see how there can be
Exceptions, even to this, this firmament, graciousness that is home?

CAESURA

Job sat in a corner of the dump eating asparagus
With one hand and scratching his unsightly eruptions
With the other. Pshaw, it'd blow over. In the office
They'd like discussing it. His thoughts

Were with the office now: how protected it was,
Though still a place to work. Sit up straight, the
Monitor inside said. It worked for a second
But didn't improve the posture of his days, taken

As a cross section of the times. Correction: of our time.
And it was (it was again): "Have you made your list up?
I have one ambulance three nuns two (black-
And-white list) cops dressed as Keystone Kops lists, a red light

At leafy intersection list." Then it goes blank, pulp-color.
Until at the end where they give out the list
Of awardees. The darkness and light have returned. It was still
The weather of the soul, vandalized, out-at-elbow. A blight. Spared,
though.

THE LEASING OF SEPTEMBER

The sleeping map lay green, and we who were never much
To begin with, except for what the attractiveness of youth
Contributed, stood around in the pastures of heaped-up, thickened
White light, convinced that the story was coming to a close,

Otherwise why all these figurines, the Latin freemasonry in the
  corners?
You stepped into a blue taxi, and as I swear my eyes were in keeping
With the beauty of you as they saw it, so a swallow perpetuated
In dove-gray dusk can be both the end and the exaltation of a new

Beginning, yet forever remain itself, as you
Seem to run alongside me as the car picks up speed. Is it
Your hand then? Will I always then return
To the tier upon tier of cloth layered in the closet

Against what departure? Even a departure from the normal?
So we are not recognized, under the metal. But to him
The love was a solid object, like a partly unpacked trunk,
As it was then, which is different now when remembered.

ON THE TERRACE OF INGOTS

It was the bitterness of the last time
That only believers and fools take for the next time
Proposing itself as a chore against an expressionist
Backdrop of skylights and other believed finial flourishes, and

You wash your hands, become a duct to drain off
All the suffering of the age you thought you had
Put behind you in defining it, but the sense mounts
Slowly in the words as in a hygrometer—that day

You stood apart from the class in the photograph.
The trees seemed to make a little sense, more precious
Than anything on earth. For the clamor
Was drawing it all away, as in a parade; you saw

How much smaller it all kept getting. And the fathers
Failed. I don't think it would be different today
If we are alone up here. The flares of today
Aren't like suffering either, yet are almost everyone.

TIDE MUSIC

Again in the autumn there is a case for it,
The tastelessness that just curls up and sometimes dies
At the edge of certain thoughtful, uneventful sidewalks.
In the afternoon you can hear what you can't see, all around,

The patterns of distress settling into rings
Of warm self-satisfaction and disbelief, as though
The whole surface of the air and the morrow were scored
Over and over with a nail as heavy rains

Pounded the area, until underneath all was revealed as mild,
Transient shining, the way a cloud dissolves
Around the light that is of its own making, hard as it is
To believe, and as though the welcoming host in you had

For some reason left the door to the street open and all
Kinds of amiable boors had taken advantage of it, though the mat
Isn't out. All the sky, each ragged leaf, have been thoroughly
   gone over
And every inch is accounted for in the tune, the wallpaper of dreams.

UNUSUAL PRECAUTIONS

"We, we children, why our lives are circumscribed, circumferential;
Close, too close to the center, we are haunted by perimeters
And our lives seem to go in and out, in and out all the time,
As though yours were diagonal, vertical, shallow, chopped off

At the root like the voice of the famous gadfly: 'Oh! Aho!' it
Sits in the middle of the roadway. That's it. Worry and brown desk
Stain it by infusion. There aren't enough tags at the end,
And the grove is blind, blossoming, but we are too porous to hear it.

It's like watching a movie of a nightmare, the many episodes
That defuse the thrust of what comes to us. The girl who juggled
  Indian clubs
Belongs again to the paper space that backs the black
Curtain, as though there were a reason to have paid for these
  seats.

Tomorrow you'll be walking in a white park. Our interests
Are too close for us to see. There seems to be no
Necessity for it, yet in walking, we too, around, and all around
We'll come to one, where the street crosses your name, and feet
  run up it."

FLOW BLUE

It may sound like a lot of odds and cloud-filled
Ends—at best, a thinking man's charmed fragment, perhaps
A house. And it could be that father and sky—
Moments so far gone into decay, as well as barely

Rating entry into a stonemason's yard—from the very first moment
Need no persuading: we know that the sky sits,
That these are sculptures of singular detail
Separate to a particular society. The black jell-like

Substance pours from the eye into the tower in the field,
Making uneasy acceptance. There were differences when
Only you knew them, and the grass was gray, escaping the houses,
The septic tank and the fields. Lost, I found the small stand

In the wood. It was funny and quiet there. And I know now how
This is not a place where I could stay. The endless ladder being carried
Past our affairs, like strings in a hop-field, decants
A piano-tuning we feed on as it dances us to the edge.

HARD TIMES

Trust me. The world is run on a shoestring.
They have no time to return the calls in hell
And pay dearly for those wasted minutes. Somewhere
In the future it will filter down through all the proceedings

But by then it will be too late, the festive ambience
Will linger on but it won't matter. More or less
Succinctly they will tell you what we've all known for years:
That the power of this climate is only to conserve itself.

Whatever twists around it is decoration and can never
Be looked at as something isolated, apart. Get it? And
He flashed a mouthful of aluminum teeth there in the darkness
To tell however it gets down, that it does, at last.

Once they made the great trip to California
And came out of it flushed. And now every day
Will have to dispel the notion of being like all the others.
In time, it gets to stand with the wind, but by then the night is
closed off.

"MOI, JE SUIS LA TULIPE . . ."

And you get two of everything. Twin tunics, the blue
And the faded. And are wise for today, allowing as how people,
Dressing up in their way, will repeat your blunder out of kindness
So it won't happen again. Seriously, the magazines speak of you,

Mention you, a lot. I have seen the articles and the ads recently.
Your name is on everyone's lips. Nobody comes to see us, because
You have to forget yourself in order to forget other people,
At which point the game is under way. My personality fades away

As dreams evaporate by day, which stays, with the dream
Materials in solution, cast out in a fiery precipitate
Later with people on their way, on parade in a way, and all kinds
Of things. All men are ambiguous and

They sometimes have hairy chests, in a long line
Of decayed and decaying ancestors. Fine in my time, I
Know that I am still, but that there is a blur around
The hole that hatches me into reason, surprised, somewhat, but sure.

CATALPAS

All around us an extraordinary effort is being made.
Something is in the air. The tops of trees are trying
To speak to this. The audience for these events is amazed,
Can't believe them, yet is walking in its sleep,

By twos and threes, on the ramparts in the moonlight.
Understanding must be introduced now, at no matter what cost.
Nature wants us to understand in many ways
That the age of noyades is over, although danger still lurks

In the enormous effrontery that appearances put on things,
And will continue to for some time. But all this comes as no surprise;
You knew the plot before, and expected to arrive in this place
At the appointed time, and now it's almost over, even

As it's erupting in huge blankets of forms and solemn,
Candy-colored ideas that you recognize as your own,
Only they look so strange up there on the stage, like the light
That shines through sleep. And the third day ends.

WE HESITATE

The days to come are a watershed.
You have to improve your portrait of God
To make it plain. It is on the list,
You and your bodies are on the line.

The new past now unfurls like a great somber hope
Above the treeline, like a giant's hand
Placed tentatively on the hurrying clouds.
The basins come to be full and complex

But it is not enough. Concern and embarrassment
Grow rank. Once they have come home there is no cursing.
Fires disturb the evening. No one can hear the story.
Or sometimes people just forget

Like a child. It took me months
To get that discipline banned, and what is the use,
To ban that? You remain a sane, yet sophisticated, person:
Rooted in twilight, dreaming, a piece of traffic.

THE DESPERADO

What kind of life is this that we are leading
That so much strong vagary can slip by unnoticed?
Is there a future? It seems that all we'd planned
To find in it is rolling around now, spending itself.

You step aside, and the rock invasion from the fifties
Dissipates in afternoon smoke. And disco
Retreats a little, wiping large brown eyes.
They come along here. Now, all will be gone.

I am the shadowed, widower, the unconsoled.
But if it weren't for me I should also be the schoolmaster
Coaching, pruning young spring thoughts
Surprised to be here, in this air.

But their barely restrained look suits the gray
Importance of what we expect to be confronted with
Any day. Send the odious one a rebuke. Can one deny
Any longer that it is, and going to be?

THE IMAGE OF THE SHARK CONFRONTS THE IMAGE OF THE LITTLE MATCH GIRL

With a stool on your head you
Again find yourself in that narrow alley
That threads the whole center of the city.
"*They're not nice people today is not nice*"

Is the austere bleat and the helpful hints
On the back are overlooked, just as before.
I know whose agents have set feet on this way,
This time. And the sky is unforgettable.

Take a sip of your mother's drink. It was told
Long ago in the Borodin string quartet how the mists
And certain other parts of antediluvian forests still
Hassle this downtown mysteriously, and sometimes

The voice of reason is heard for a hard, clear moment,
Then falls still, if for no other reason than
That the sheriff's deputies have suddenly coincided
With a collective notion of romance, and the minute has absconded.

SONGS WITHOUT WORDS

Yes, we had gone down to the shore
That year and were waiting for the expected to happen
According to a preordained system of its own devising.
Its people were there for decoration,

Like notes arranged on a staff. What you made of them
Depended on your ability to read music and to hear more
In the night behind them. It gave us
A kind of amplitude. And the watchmen were praying

So long before rosy-fingered dawn began to mess around
With the horizon that you wondered, yet
It made a convenient bridge to pass over, from starlight
To the daylit kingdom. I don't think it would have been any different

If the ships hadn't been there, poised, flexing their muscles,
Ready to take us where they pleased and that country had been
Rehabilitated and the sirens, la la, stopped singing
And canceled our melting protection from the sun.

INDELIBLE, INEDIBLE

Work had been proceeding at a snail's pace
Along the river, and now that the spring torrents had begun
We kept our distance from the mitered flashing,
The easy spoke-movement of the hopeless expanse

Caught, way out in the distance, with a thread of meaning
Which was fear. Some things are always left undecided
And regroup, to reappear next year in a new light,
The light of change. And the moods are similar

Too the second time around, only more easy of access.
You can talk to each other, sheltered now,
As though just inside the flap of a big circus tent
And leave whenever you want to. Nothing could be easier.

That was then. And its enduring lasted through many
Transformations, before it came to seem as though it could not
  be done.
Cats were curious about it. They followed it
Down into the glen where it was last seen.

SCHOOL OF VELOCITY

Urban propinquities extrude a wood-pegged
(In the imperialist taste) balcony just above
The heads of penitents as their parade
Turns the corner and is seen no more. Coleridge-Taylor

Or a hare-shaped person is somehow involved;
His aquarelle takes on meaning, and a cloud
Is suddenly torn asunder so that the green heartbreak
Of the eternally hysterical sun hoses down the gutters

And tender walkways where we first became aware
Of a confession and trees that were on one side only.
Probably they wear out the light with too much fussing
Otherwise and yet the landscape looks strangely neglected.

An orphan. We are overheard,
As usual. We're sorry, I say. The houses, the puddles,
Even the cars are pegs. One who noticed the street flooded
Calls out in time. Tomorrow the procession returns, and what then?

FRONTISPIECE

Expecting rain, the profile of a day
Wears its soul like a hat, prow up
Against the deeply incised clouds and regions
Of abrupt skidding from cold to cold, riddles

Of climate it cannot understand.
Sometimes toward the end
A look of longing broke, taut, from those eyes
Meeting yours in final understanding, late,

And often, too, the beginnings went unnoticed
As though the story could advance its pawns
More discreetly thus, overstepping
The confines of ordinary health and reason

To introduce in another way
Its fact into the picture. It registered,
It must be there. And so we turn the page over
To think of starting. This is all there is.

EVERYMAN'S LIBRARY

. . . the sparrow hath found an house,
and the swallow a nest for herself . . .
PSALM 84

In the outlying districts where we know something
The sparrows don't, and each house
Is noticeably a little nicer than the rest, the "package"
Is ready to be performed now. It comes

As a sheaf of papyruslike, idle imaginings
And identifyings, and stays put like that.
It's beginning to get darker. You send someone
Down the flight of stairs to ask after

The true course of events and the answer always
Comes back evasive yet polite: you have only to step down . . .
Oops, the light went out. That is the paper-thin
But very firm dimension of ordinary education. And when a thief

Is out there, in the dark somewhere, it also applies.
There is no freedom, and no freedom from freedom.
The only possible act is to pick up the book, caress it
And open it in my face. You knew that.

SHADOW TRAIN

Violence, how smoothly it came
And smoothly took you with it
To wanting what you nonetheless did not want.
It's all over if we don't see the truth inside that meaning.

To want is to be better than before. To desire what is
Forbidden is permitted. But to desire it
And not want it is to chew its name like a rag.
To that end the banana shakes on its stem,

But the strawberry is liquid and cool, a rounded
Note in the descending scale, a photograph
Of someone smiling at a funeral. The great plumes
Of the dynastic fly-whisk lurch daily

Above our heads, as far up as clouds. Who can say
What it means, or whether it protects? Yet it is clear
That history merely stretches today into one's private guignol.
The violence dreams. You are half-asleep at your instrument table.

BUT NOT THAT ONE

The works, the days, uh,
And weariness of the days
Gradually getting a little longer,
Turning out to be a smile, everything

Like that. And it does make a difference,
Oh it does. Because the smile is a different not us,
Ready to rescind, cancel,
Rip out the stitches of the sky,

Then it warmed up. O a lot
Blooms, gets squashed on the tongue:
Where are you going? Who do you think you are?
Crushed leaves, berries, the stars

Continually falling, streaking the sky:
Can it be the context? No, it is old and
Sometimes the agog spectator wrenches a cry
From its own house. He thought he heard.

THE VEGETARIANS

In front of you, long tables leading down to the sun,
A great gesture building. You accept it so as to play with it
And translate when its attention is deflated for the one second
Of eternity. Extreme patience and persistence are required,

Yet everybody succeeds at this before being handed
The surprise box lunch of the rest of his life. But what is
Truly startling is that it all happens modestly in the vein of
True living, and then that too is translated into something

Floating up from it, signals that life flashed, weak but essential
For uncorking the tone, and now lost, recently but forever.
In Zurich everything was pure and purposeful, like the red cars
Swung around the lake on wires, against the sky, then back down

Through the weather. Which resembles what you want to do
No more than black tree trunks do, though you thought of it.
Therefore our legends always come around to seeming legendary,
A path decorated with our comings and goings. Or so I've been told.

A WAVE

AT NORTH FARM

Somewhere someone is traveling furiously toward you,
At incredible speed, traveling day and night,
Through blizzards and desert heat, across torrents, through
narrow passes.
But will he know where to find you,
Recognize you when he sees you,
Give you the thing he has for you?

Hardly anything grows here,
Yet the granaries are bursting with meal,
The sacks of meal piled to the rafters.
The streams run with sweetness, fattening fish;
Birds darken the sky. Is it enough
That the dish of milk is set out at night,
That we think of him sometimes,
Sometimes and always, with mixed feelings?

RAIN MOVING IN

The blackboard is erased in the attic
And the wind turns up the light of the stars,
Sinewy now. Someone will find out, someone will know.
And if somewhere on this great planet
The truth is discovered, a patch of it, dried, glazed by the sun,
It will just hang on, in its own infamy, humility. No one
Will be better for it, but things can't get any worse.
Just keep playing, mastering as you do the step
Into disorder this one meant. Don't you see
It's all we can do? Meanwhile, great fires
Arise, as of haystacks aflame. The dial has been set
And that's ominous, but all your graciousness in living
Conspires with it, now that this is our home:
A place to be from, and have people ask about.

THE SONGS WE KNOW BEST

Just like a shadow in an empty room
Like a breeze that's pointed from beyond the tomb
Just like a project of which no one tells—
Or didja really think that I was somebody else?

Your clothes and pantlegs lookin' out of shape
Shape of the body over which they drape
Body which has acted in so many scenes
But didja ever think of what that body means?

It is an organ and a vice to some
A necessary evil which we all must shun
To others an abstraction and a piece of meat
But when you're looking out you're in the driver's seat!

No man cares little about fleshly things
They fill him with a silence that spreads in rings
We wish to know more but we are never sated
No wonder some folks think the flesh is overrated!

The things we know now all got learned in school
Try to learn a new thing and you break the rule
Our knowledge isn't much it's just a small amount
But you feel it quick inside you when you're down for the count

You look at me and frown like I was out of place
I guess I never did much for the human race
Just hatched some schemes on paper that looked good at first
Sat around and watched until the bubble burst

And now you're lookin' good all up and down the line
Except for one thing you still have in mind

It's always there though often with a different face
It's the worm inside the jumping bean that makes it race

Too often when you thought you'd be showered with confetti
What they flung at you was a plate of hot spaghetti
You've put your fancy clothes and flashy gems in hock
Yet you pause before your father's door afraid to knock

Once you knew the truth it tried to set you free
And still you stood transfixed just like an apple tree
The truth it came and went and left you in the lurch
And now you think you see it from your lofty perch

The others come and go they're just a dime a dozen
You react to them no more than to a distant cousin
Only a few people can touch your heart
And they too it seems have all gotten a false start

In twilight the city with its hills shines serene
And lets you make of it more than anything could mean
It's the same city by day that seems so crude and calm
You'll have to get to know it not just pump its arm

Even when that bugle sounded loud and clear
You knew it put an end to all your fear
To all that lying and the senseless mistakes
And now you've got it right and you know what it takes

Someday I'll look you up when we're both old and gray
And talk about those times we had so far away
How much it mattered then and how it matters still
Only things look so different when you've got a will

It's true that out of this misunderstanding could end
And men would greet each other like they'd found a friend
With lots of friends around there's no one to entice
And don't you think seduction isn't very nice?

It carries in this room against the painted wall
And hangs in folds of curtains when it's not there at all
It's woven in the flowers of the patterned spread
And lies and knows not what it thinks upon the bed

I wish to come to know you get to know you all
Let your belief in me and me in you stand tall
Just like a project of which no one tells—
Or do ya still think that I'm somebody else?

WHEN THE SUN WENT DOWN

To have been loved once by someone—surely
There is a permanent good in that,
Even if we don't know all the circumstances
Or it happened too long ago to make any difference.
Like almost too much sunlight or an abundance of sweet-sticky,
Caramelized things—who can tell you it's wrong?
Which of the others on your team could darken the passive
Melody that runs on, that has been running since the world began?

Yet, to be strapped to one's mindset, which seems
As enormous as a plain, to have to be told
That its horizons are comically confining,
And all the sorrow wells from there, like the slanting
Plume of a waterspout: doesn't it supplant knowledge
Of the different forms of love, reducing them
To a white indifferent prism, a roofless love standing open
To the elements? And some see in this a paradigm of how it rises
Slowly to the indifferent heavens, all that pale glamour?

The refrain is desultory as birdsong; it seeps unrecognizably
Into the familiar structures that lead out from here
To the still familiar peripheries and less sure notions:
It already had its way. In time for evening relaxation.
There are times when music steals a march on us,
Is suddenly perplexingly nearer, flowing in my wrist;
Is the true and dirty words you whisper nightly
As the book closes like a collapsing sheet, a blur
Of all kinds of connotations ripped from the hour and tossed
Like jewels down a well; the answer, also,
To the question that was on my mind but that I've forgotten,
Except in the way certain things, certain nights, come together.

LANDSCAPE
(After Baudelaire)

I want a bedroom near the sky, an astrologer's cave
Where I can fashion eclogues that are chaste and grave.
Dreaming, I'll hear the wind in the steeples close by
Sweep the solemn hymns away. I'll spy
On factories from my attic window, resting my chin
In both hands, drinking in the songs, the din.
I'll see chimneys and steeples, those masts of the city,
And the huge sky that makes us dream of eternity.

How sweet to watch the birth of the star in the still-blue
Sky, through mist; the lamp burning anew
At the window; rivers of coal climbing the firmament
And the moon pouring out its pale enchantment.
I'll see the spring, the summer and the fall
And when winter casts its monotonous pall
Of snow, I'll draw the blinds and curtains tight
And build my magic palaces in the night;
Then dream of gardens, of bluish horizons,
Of jets of water weeping in alabaster basins,
Of kisses, of birds singing at dawn and at nightfall,
Of all that's most childish in our pastoral.
When the storm rattles my windowpane
I'll stay hunched at my desk, it will roar in vain
For I'll have plunged deep inside the thrill
Of conjuring spring with the force of my will,
Coaxing the sun from my heart, and building here
Out of my fiery thoughts, a tepid atmosphere.

JUST WALKING AROUND

What name do I have for you?
Certainly there is no name for you
In the sense that the stars have names
That somehow fit them. Just walking around,

An object of curiosity to some,
But you are too preoccupied
By the secret smudge in the back of your soul
To say much, and wander around,

Smiling to yourself and others.
It gets to be kind of lonely
But at the same time off-putting,
Counterproductive, as you realize once again

That the longest way is the most efficient way,
The one that looped among islands, and
You always seemed to be traveling in a circle
And now that the end is near

The segments of the trip swing open like an orange.
There is light in there, and mystery and food.
Come see it. Come not for me but it.
But if I am still there, grant that we may see each other.

A FLY

And still I automatically look to that place on the wall—
The timing is right, but off—
The approval soured—
That's what comes of age but not aging,
The marbles all snapped into the side pockets,
The stance for today we know full well is
Yesterday's delivery and ripe prediction—
The way not to hold in when circling,
As a delighted draughtsman sits down to his board.

Reasons, reasons for this:
The enthusiast mopping through his hair again
As he squats on the toilet and catches one eye in the mirror
(Guys it has come through all right
For once as delivered it's all here and me with time on my hands
For once, with writing to spare, and how many
Times have there been words to waste,
That you had to spend or else take big losses
In the car after an early dinner the endless
Light streaking out of the windshield
A breakthrough
I guess but don't just now take into account,
Don't look at the time) and time
Comes looking for you, out of Pennsylvania and New Jersey
It doesn't travel well
Colors his hair beige
Paints the straw walls gilds the mirror

The thing is that this is places in the world,
Freedom from rent,
Sundries, food, a dictionary to keep you company
Enviously
But is also the day we all got together

That the treaty was signed
And it all eased off into the big afternoon off the coast
Slid shoulders into the groundswell removed its boots
That we may live now with some
Curiosity and hope
Like pools that soon become part of the tide

THE ONGOING STORY

I could say it's the happiest period of my life.
It hasn't got much competition! Yesterday
It seemed a flatness, hotness. As though it barely stood out
From the rocks of all the years before. Today it sheds
That old name, without assuming any new one. I think it's still there.

It was as though I'd been left with the empty street
A few seconds after the bus pulled out. A dollop of afternoon wind.
Others tell you to take your attention off it
For awhile, refocus the picture. Plan to entertain,
To get out. (Do people really talk that way?)

We could pretend that all that isn't there never existed anyway.
The great ideas? What good are they if they're misplaced,
In the wrong order, if you can't remember one
At the moment you're so to speak mounting the guillotine
Like Sydney Carton, and can't think of anything to say?
Or is this precisely material covered in a course
Called Background of the Great Ideas, and therefore it isn't necessary
To say anything or even know anything? The breath of the moment
Is breathed, we fall and still feel better. The phone rings,

It's a wrong number, and your heart is lighter,
Not having to be faced with the same boring choices again
Which doesn't undermine a feeling for people in general and
Especially in particular: you,
In your deliberate distinctness, whom I love and gladly
Agree to walk blindly into the night with,
Your realness is real to me though I would never take any of it
Just to see how it grows. A knowledge that people live close by is,
I think, enough. And even if only first names are ever exchanged
The people who own them seem rock-true and marvelously
  self-sufficient.

THANK YOU FOR NOT COOPERATING

Down in the street there are ice-cream parlors to go to
And the pavement is a nice, bluish slate-gray. People laugh a lot.
Here you can see the stars. Two lovers are singing
Separately, from the same rooftop: "*Leave your change behind.*
Leave your clothes, and go. It is time now.
It was time before too, but now it is really time.
You will never have enjoyed storms so much
As on these hot sticky evenings that are more like August
Than September. Stay. A fake wind wills you to go
And out there on the stormy river witness buses bound for
  Connecticut,
And tree-business, and all that we think about when we stop thinking.
The weather is perfect, the season unclear. Weep for your going
But also expect to meet me in the near future, when I shall disclose
New further adventures, and that you shall continue to think of me."

The wind dropped, and the lovers
Sang no more, communicating each to each in the tedium
Of self-expression, and the shore curled up and became liquid
And so the celebrated lament began. And how shall we, people
All unused to each other and to our own business, explain
It to the shore if it is given to us
To circulate there "in the near future" the why of our coming
And why we were never here before? The counterproposals
Of the guest-stranger impede our construing of ourselves as
Person-objects, the ones we knew would get here
Somehow, but we can remember as easily as the day we were born
The maggots we passed on the way and how the day bled
And the night too on hearing us, though we spoke only our childish
Ideas and never tried to impress anybody even when somewhat older.

BUT WHAT IS THE READER TO MAKE OF THIS?

A lake of pain, an absence
Leading to a flowering sea? Give it a quarter-turn
And watch the centuries begin to collapse
Through each other, like floors in a burning building,
Until we get to this afternoon:

Those delicious few words spread around like jam
Don't matter, nor does the shadow.
We have lived blasphemously in history
And nothing has hurt us or can.
But beware of the monstrous tenderness, for out of it
The same blunt archives loom. Facts seize hold of the web
And leave it ash. Still, it is the personal,
Interior life that gives us something to think about.
The rest is only drama.

Meanwhile the combinations of every extendable circumstance
In our lives continue to blow against it like new leaves
At the edge of a forest a battle rages in and out of
For a whole day. It's not the background, we're the background,
On the outside looking out. The surprises history has
For us are nothing compared to the shock we get
From each other, though time still wears
The colors of meanness and melancholy, and the general life
Is still many sizes too big, yet
Has style, woven of things that never happened
With those that did, so that a mood survives
Where life and death never could. Make it sweet again!

DOWN BY THE STATION, EARLY IN THE MORNING

It all wears out. I keep telling myself this, but
I can never believe me, though others do. Even things do.
And the things they do. Like the rasp of silk, or a certain
Glottal stop in your voice as you are telling me how you
Didn't have time to brush your teeth but gargled with Listerine
Instead. Each is a base one might wish to touch once more

Before dying. There's the moment years ago in the station in Venice,
The dark rainy afternoon in fourth grade, and the shoes then,
Made of a dull crinkled brown leather that no longer exists.
And nothing does, until you name it, remembering, and even then
It may not have existed, or existed only as a result
Of the perceptual dysfunction you've been carrying around for years.
The result is magic, then terror, then pity at the emptiness,
Then air gradually bathing and filling the emptiness as it leaks,
Emoting all over something that is probably mere reportage
But nevertheless likes being emoted on. And so each day
Culminates in merriment as well as a deep shock like an electric one,

As the wrecking ball bursts through the wall with the bookshelves
Scattering the works of famous authors as well as those
Of more obscure ones, and books with no author, letting in
Space, and an extraneous babble from the street
Confirming the new value the hollow core has again, the light
From the lighthouse that protects as it pushes us away.

AROUND THE ROUGH AND RUGGED ROCKS THE RAGGED RASCAL RUDELY RAN

I think a lot about it,
Think quite a lot about it—
The omnipresent possibility of being interrupted
While what I stand for is still almost a bare canvas:
A few traceries, that may be fibers, perhaps
Not even these but shadows, hallucinations. . . .

And it is well then to recall
That this track is the outer rim of a flat crust,
Dimensionless, except for its poor, parched surface,
The face one raises to God,
Not the rich dark composite
We keep to ourselves,
Carpentered together any old way,
Coffee from an old tin can, a belch of daylight,
People leaving the beach.
If I could write it
And also write about it—
The interruption—
Rudeness on the face of it, but who
Knows anything about our behavior?

Forget what it is you're coming out of,
Always into something like a landscape
Where no one has ever walked
Because they're too busy.
Excitedly you open your rhyming dictionary.
It has begun to snow.

MORE PLEASANT ADVENTURES

The first year was like icing.
Then the cake started to show through.
Which was fine, too, except you forget the direction you're taking.
Suddenly you are interested in some new thing
And can't tell how you got here. Then there is confusion
Even out of happiness, like a smoke—
The words get heavy, some topple over, you break others.
And outlines disappear once again.

Heck, it's anybody's story,
A sentimental journey—"gonna take a sentimental journey,"
And we do, but you wake up under the table of a dream:
You are that dream, and it is the seventh layer of you.
We haven't moved an inch, and everything has changed.
We are somewhere near a tennis court at night.
We get lost in life, but life knows where we are.
We can always be found with our associates.
Haven't you always wanted to curl up like a dog and go to sleep
  like a dog?

In the rash of partings and dyings (the new twist),
There's also room for breaking out of living.
Whatever happens will be quite ingenious.
No acre but will resume being disputed now,
And paintings are one thing we never seem to run out of.

PURISTS WILL OBJECT

We have the looks you want:
The gonzo (musculature seemingly wired to the stars);
Colors like lead, khaki and pomegranate; things you
Put in your hair, with the whole panoply of the past:
Landscape embroidery, complete sets of this and that.
It's bankruptcy, the human haul,
The shining, bulging nets lifted out of the sea, and always a
few refugees
Dropping back into the no-longer-mirthful kingdom
On the day someone sells an old house
And someone else begins to add on to his: all
In the interests of this pornographic masterpiece,
Variegated, polluted skyscraper to which all gazes are drawn,
Pleasure we cannot and will not escape.

It seems we were going home.
The smell of blossoming privet blanketed the narrow avenue.
The traffic lights were green and aqueous.
So this is the subterranean life.
If it can't be conjugated onto us, what good is it?
What need for purists when the demotic is built to last,
To outlast us, and no dialect hears us?

DESCRIPTION OF A MASQUE

The persimmon velvet curtain rose swiftly to reveal a space of uncertain dimensions and perspective. As the lower left was a grotto, the cave of Mania, goddess of confusion. Larches, alders and Douglas fir were planted so thickly around the entrance that one could scarcely make it out. In the dooryard a hyena chained to a pole slunk back and forth, back and forth, continually measuring the length of its chain, emitting the well-known laughing sound all the while, except at intervals when what appeared to be fragments of speech would issue from its maw. It was difficult to hear the words, let alone understand them, though now and then a phrase like "Up your arse!" or "Turn the rascals out!" could be distinguished for a moment, before subsiding into a confused chatter. Close by the entrance to the grotto was a metal shoescraper in the form of a hyena, and very like this particular one, whose fur was a grayish-white faintly tinged with pink, and scattered over with foul, liver-colored spots. On the other side of the dooryard opposite the hyena's pole was a graceful statue of Mercury on a low, gilded pedestal, facing out toward the audience with an expression of delighted surprise on his face. The statue seemed to be made of lead or some other dull metal, painted an off-white which had begun to flake in places, revealing the metal beneath which was of almost the same color. As yet there was no sign of the invisible proprietress of the grotto.

A little to the right and about eight feet above this scene, another seemed to hover in mid-air. It suggested the interior of an English pub, as it might be imitated in Paris. Behind the bar, opposite the spectators in the audience, was a mural adapted from a Tenniel illustration for *Through the Looking-Glass*—the famous one in which a fish in a footman's livery holds out a large envelope to a frog footman who has just emerged onto the front stoop of a small house, while in the background, partially concealed by the trunk of a tree, Alice lurks, an expression of amusement on her face. Time and the fumes of a public house had darkened the colors almost to a rich mahogany glow, and if one had not known the illustration it would have been difficult to make out some of the details.

Seven actors and actresses, representing seven nursery-rhyme characters, populated the scene. Behind the bar the bald barman, Georgie Porgie, stood motionless, gazing out at the audience. In front and a little to his left, lounging on a tall stool, was Little Jack Horner, in fact quite a tall and roguish-looking young man wearing a trench coat and expensive blue jeans; he had placed his camera on the bar near him. He too faced out toward the audience. In front of him, his back to the audience, Little Boy Blue partially knelt before him, apparently performing an act of fellatio on him. Boy Blue was entirely clothed in blue denim, of an ordinary kind.

To their left, Simple Simon and the Pie Man stood facing each other in profile. The Pie Man's gaze was directed toward the male couple at the center of the bar; at the same time he continually offered and withdrew a pie coveted by Simon, whose attention was divided between the pie and the scene behind him, at which he kept glancing over his shoulder, immediately turning back toward the pie as the Pie Man withdrew it, Simon all the time pretending to fumble in his pocket for a penny. The Pie Man was dressed like a French baker's apprentice, in a white blouse and blue-and-white checked pants; he appeared to be about twenty-eight years of age. Simon was about the same age, but he was wearing a Buster Brown outfit, with a wide-brimmed hat, dark blue blazer and short pants, and a large red bow tie.

At the opposite end of the bar sat two young women, their backs to the audience, apparently engaged in conversation. The first, Polly Flinders, was wearing a strapless dress of ash-colored chiffon with a narrow silver belt. She sat closest to Jack Horner and Boy Blue, but paid no attention to them and turned frequently toward her companion, at the same time puffing on a cigarette in a shiny black cigarette holder and sipping a martini straight up with an olive. Daffy Down Dilly, the other young woman, had long straight blond hair which had obviously been brushed excessively so that it gleamed when it caught the light; it was several shades of blond in easily distinguishable streaks. She wore a long emerald-green velvet gown cut very low in back, and held up by glittering rhinestone straps; her yellow lace-edged petticoat hung down about an inch and a half below the hem of her gown. She did not smoke but from time to time sipped through a straw on a whiskey sour, also straight up. Although she frequently faced in the direction of the other characters when she turned toward Polly, she too paid them no mind.

After a few moments Jack seemed to grow weary of Boy Blue's attentions and gave him a brisk shove which sent him sprawling on the floor, where he walked about on all fours barking like a dog for several minutes, causing the hyena in the bottom left tableau to stop its own prowling and fall silent except for an occasional whimper, as though wondering where the barking was coming from. Soon Boy Blue curled up in front of the bar and pretended to fall asleep, resting his head on the brass rail, and the hyena continued as before. Jack rearranged his clothing and turned toward the barman, who handed him another drink. At this point the statue of Mercury stepped from its pedestal and seemed to float upward into the bar scene, landing on tiptoe between Jack and Simple Simon. After a deep bow in the direction of the ladies, who ignored him, he turned to face the audience and delivered the following short speech.

"My fellow prisoners, we have no idea how long each of us has been in this town and how long each of us intends to stay, although I have reason to believe that the lady in green over there is a fairly recent arrival. My point, however, is this. Instead of loitering this way, we should all become part of a collective movement, get involved with each other and with our contemporaries on as many levels as possible. No one will disagree that there is much to be gained from contact with one another, and I, as a god, feel it even more keenly than you do. My understanding, though universal, lacks the personal touch and the local color which would make it meaningful to me."

These words seemed to produce an uneasiness among the other patrons of the bar. Even Little Boy Blue stopped pretending to be asleep and glanced warily at the newcomer. The two girls had left off conversing. After a few moments Daffy got down off her bar stool and walked over to Mercury. Opening a green brocade pocketbook, she pulled out a small revolver and shot him in the chest. The bullet passed through him without harming him and imbedded itself in the fish in the mural behind the bar, causing it to lurch forward regurgitating blood and drop the envelope, which produced a loud report and a flash like a magnesium flare that illuminated an expression of anger and fear on Alice's face, as she hastily clapped her hands over her ears. Then the whole stage was plunged in darkness, the last thing remaining visible being the apparently permanent smile on Mercury's face—still astonished and delighted, and bearing no trace of malice.

Little by little the darkness began to dissipate, and a forest scene similar to that in the mural was revealed. It had moved forward to fill the space formerly occupied by the bar and its customers, and was much neater and tidier than the forest in the mural had been. The trees were more or less the same size and shape, and planted equidistant from each other. There was no forest undergrowth, no dead leaves or rotting tree trunks on the ground; the grass under the trees was as green and well kept as that of a lawn. This was because the scene represented a dream of Mania (whose grotto was still visible in the lower left-hand corner of the stage), and, since she was the goddess of confusion, her dream revealed no trace of confusion, or at any rate presented a confusing absence of confusion. On a white banner threaded through some of the branches of the trees in the foreground the sentence "It's an On-going Thing" was printed in scarlet letters. To the left, toward the rear of the scene, Alice appeared to be asleep at the base of a tree trunk, with a pig dressed in baby clothes asleep in her lap. An invisible orchestra in the pit intoned the "March" from Grieg's *Sigurd Jorsalfar*. A group of hobos who had previously been hidden behind the trees moved to the center of the stage and began to perform a slow-moving ballet to the music. Each was dressed identically in baggy black-and-white checked trousers held up by white suspenders fastened with red buttons, a crumpled black swallowtail coat, red flannel undershirt, brown derby hat and white gloves with black stripes outlining the contours of the wrist bones, and each held in his right hand an extinguished cigar butt with a fat gray puffy ash affixed to it. Moving delicately on point, the group formed an ever-narrowing semicircle around Alice and the sleeping pig, when a sudden snort from the latter startled them and each disappeared behind a tree. At this moment Mania emerged from her grotto dressed in a gown of sapphire-blue tulle studded with blue sequins, cradling a sheaf of white gladioli in the crook of one arm and with her other hand holding aloft a wand with a gilt cardboard star at its tip. Only her curiously unkempt hair marred the somewhat dated elegance of her toilette. Deftly detaching the hyena's chain from its post, she allowed the beast to lead her upward to the forest scene where the hobos had each begun to peek out from behind his tree trunk. Like the Wilis in *Giselle*, they appeared mesmerized by the apparition of the goddess, swaying to the movement of her star-tipped wand as she waved it, describing wide arcs around herself. None dared draw too close, however, for if they did so the snarling, slavering hyena would lurch forward, straining at its chain. At length she let her wand droop toward the ground, and after gazing pensively downward for some moments she raised her head and, tossing back her matted curls, spoke thus:

"My sister *Hecat*, who sometimes accompanies me on midnight rides to nameless and indescribable places, warned me of this dell, seemingly laid out for the Sunday strolls of civil servants, but in reality the haunt of drifters and retarded children. *You*," she cried, shaking her wand at the corps de ballet of hobos, who stumbled and fell over each other in their frantic attempt to get away from her, "you who oppress even my dreams, where a perverse order should reign but where I find instead traces of the lunacy that besets my waking hours, are accomplices in all this, comical and ineffectual though you pretend to be. As for that creature" (here she gestured toward the sleeping Alice), "she knows only too well the implications of her presence here with that changeling, and how these constitute a reflection on my inward character as illustrated in my outward appearance, such as this spangled gown and these tangled tresses, meant to epitomize the confusion which is the one source of my living being, but which in these ambiguous surroundings, neither true fantasy nor clean-cut reality, keeps me at bay until I can no longer see the woman I once was. I shall not rest until I have erased all of this from my thoughts, or (which is more likely) incorporated it into the confusing scheme I have erected around me for my support and glorification."

At this there was some whispering and apprehensive regrouping among the hobos; meanwhile Alice and the pig slept on oblivious, the latter's snores having become more relaxed and peaceful than before. Mania continued to stride back and forth, impetuously stabbing her wand into the ground. Suddenly a black horse with a rider swathed in a dark cloak and with a dark sombrero pulled down over his face approached quickly along a path leading through the trees from the right of the stage. Without dismounting or revealing his face the stranger accosted the lady:

STRANGER: Why do you pace back and forth like this, ignoring the critical reality of this scene, or pretending that it is a monstrosity of reason sent by some envious commonsensical deity to confound and humiliate you? You might have been considered beautiful, and an ornament even to such a curious setting as this, had you not persisted in spoiling the clear and surprising outline of your character, and leading around this hideous misshapen beast as though to scare off any who might have approached you so as to admire you.

MANIA: I am as I am, and in that I am happy, and care nothing for the opinion of others. The very idea of the idea others might entertain of me is as a poison to me, pushing me to flee farther into wastes even less hospitable and more treacherously combined of irregular elements than this one. As for my pet hyena, beauty is in the eye of the beholder; at least, I find him beautiful, and, unlike other beasts, he has the ability to laugh and sneer at the spectacle around us.

STRANGER: Come with me, and I will take you into the presence of one at whose court beauty and irrationality reign alternately, and never tread on each other's toes as do your unsightly followers [more whispering and gesturing among the hobos], where your own pronounced contours may flourish and be judged for what they are worth, while the anomalies of the room you happen to be in or the disturbing letters and phone calls that hamper your free unorthodox development will melt away like crystal rivulets leaving a glacier, and you may dwell in the accident of your character forever.

MANIA: You speak well, and if all there is as you say, I am convinced and will accompany you gladly. But before doing so I must ask you two questions. First, what is the name of her to whose palace you purpose to lead me, and second, may I bring my hyena along?

STRANGER: As to the first question, that I may not answer now, but you'll find out soon enough. As to the second, the answer is yes, providing it behaves itself.

The lady mounted the stranger's steed with his help, and sat sideways, with the hyena on its chain trotting along behind them. As they rode back into the woods the forest faded away and the scene became an immense metallic sky in which a huge lead-colored sphere or disc—impossible to determine which—seemed to float midway between the proscenium and the floor of the stage. At right and left behind the footlights some of the hobos, reduced almost to midget size, rushed back and forth gesticulating at the strange orb that hung above them; with them mingled a few nursery-rhyme characters such as the Knave of Hearts and the Pie Man, who seemed to be looking around uneasily for Simon. All were puzzled or terrified by the strange new apparition, which seemed to grow darker and denser while the sky surrounding it stayed the same white-metal color.

Alice, awakening from her slumber, stood up and joined the group at the front of the stage, leaving the pig in its baby clothes to scamper off into the wings. Wiping away some strands of hair that had fallen across her forehead and seeming to become aware of the changed landscape around her, she turned to the others and asked, "What happens now?"

In reply, Jack Horner, who had been gazing at the camera in his hand with an expression of ironic detachment, like Hamlet contemplating the skull of Yorick, jerked his head upward toward the banner, whose scarlet motto still blazed brightly though the trees that supported it were fast fading in the glare from the sky. Alice too looked up, noticing it for the first time.

"I see," she said at length. "A process of duration has been set in motion around us, though there is no indication I can see that any of us is involved in it. If that is the case, what conclusion are we to draw? Why are we here, if even such a nebulous concept as 'here' is to be allowed us? What are we to do?"

At this the Knave of Hearts stepped forward and cast his eyes modestly toward the ground. "I see separate, soft pain, lady," he said. "The likes of these"—he indicated with a sweep of his arm the group of hobos and others who had subsided into worried reclining poses in the background—"who know not what they are, or what they mean, I isolate from the serious business of creatures such as we, both more ordinary and more distinguished than the common herd of anesthetized earthlings. It is so that we may question more acutely the sphere into which we have been thrust, that threatens to smother us at every second and above which we rise triumphant with each breath we draw. At least, that is the way I see it."

"Then you are a fool as well as a knave," Jack answered angrily, "since you don't seem to realize that the sphere is escaping us, rather than the reverse, and that in a moment it will have become one less thing to carry."

As he spoke the stage grew very dark, so that the circle in the sky finally seemed light by contrast, while a soft wail arose from the instuments in the orchestra pit.

"I suspect the mischief of Mercury in all this," muttered Jack, keeping a weather eye on the heavens. "For though some believe Hermes' lineage to be celestial, others maintain that he is of infernal origin, and emerges on earth to do the errands of Pluto and Proserpine on the rare occasions when they have business here."

The lights slowly came up again, revealing a perspective view of a busy main street in a large American city. The dark outline of the disc still persisted in the sky, yet the climate seemed warm and sunny, though there were Christmas decorations strung across the street and along the façades of department stores, and on a nearby street corner stood a Salvation Army Santa Claus with his bell and cauldron. It could have been downtown Los Angeles in the late 30s or early- to mid-40s, judging from the women's fashions and the models of cars that crawled along the street as though pulled by invisible strings.

Walking in place on a sidewalk which was actually a treadmill moving toward the back of the stage was a couple in their early thirties. Mania (for the woman was none other than she) was dressed in the style of Joan Crawford in *Mildred Pierce*, in a severe suit with padded shoulders and a pillbox with a veil crowning the pincurls of her upswept hairdo, which also cascaded to her shoulders, ending in more pincurls. Instead of the sheaf of gladioli she now clutched a black handbag suspended on a strap over her shoulder, and in place of the hyena, one of those *little white dogs* on the end of a leash kept sniffing the legs of pedestrians who were in truth mere celluloid phantoms, part of the process shot which made up the whole downtown backdrop. The man at her side wore a broad-brimmed hat, loose-fitting sport coat and baggy gabardine slacks; he bore a certain resemblance to the actor Bruce Bennett but closer inspection revealed him to be the statue of Mercury, with the paint still peeling from his face around the empty eye sockets. At first it looked as though the two were enjoying the holiday atmosphere and drinking in the sights and sounds of the city. Gradually, however, Mania's expression darkened; finally she stopped in the middle of the sidewalk and pulled at her escort's sleeve.

"Listen, Herman," she said, perhaps addressing Bruce Bennett by his real name, Herman Brix, "you said you were going to take me to this swell place and all, where I was supposed to meet a lot of interesting people who could help me in my career. All we do is walk down this dopey street looking in store windows and waiting for the stoplights to change. Is this your idea of a good time?"

"But this is all part of it, hon, part of what I promised you," Mercury rejoined. "Don't you feel the atmosphere yet? That powder-blue sky of the eternal postcard, with the haze of moun-

mountain peaks barely visible; the salmon-colored pavement with its little green and blue cars that look so still though they are supposed to be in motion? The window shoppers, people like you and me . . . ?"

"*That's* what I thought," Mania pouted, stamping one of her feet in its platform shoe so loudly that several of the extras turned to look. "Atmosphere—that's what it was all along, wasn't it? A question of ambience, poetry, something like that. I might as well have stayed in my cave for all the good it's going to do me. After all, I'm used to not blending in with the environment—it's my business not to. But I thought you were going to take me away from all that, to some place where scenery made no difference any more, where I could be what everybody accuses me of being and what I suppose I must be—my tired, tyrannical self, as separate from local color as geometry is from the hideous verticals of these avenues and buildings and the festoons that extend them into the shrinking consciousness. Have you forgotten the words of St. Augustine: 'Multiply in your imagination the light of the sun, make it greater and brighter as you will, a thousand times or out of number. God will not be there'?"

Then we all realized what should have been obvious from the start: that the setting would go on evolving eternally, rolling its waves across our vision like an ocean, each one new yet recognizably a part of the same series, which was creation itself. Scenes from movies, plays, operas, television; decisive or little-known episodes from history; prenatal and other early memories from our own solitary, separate pasts; events yet to come from life or art; calamities or moments of relaxation; universal or personal tragedies; or little vignettes from daily life that you just had to stop and laugh at, they were so funny, like the dog chasing its tail on the living-room rug. The sunny city in California faded away and another scene took its place, and another and another. And the corollary of all this was that we would go on witnessing these tableaux, not that anything prevented us from leaving the theater, but there was no alternative to our interest in finding out what would happen next. This was the only thing that mattered for us, so we stayed on although we could have stood up and walked away in disgust at any given moment. And event followed event according to an inner logic of their own. We saw the set for the first act of *La Bohème*, picturesque poverty on a scale large enough to fill the stages of the world's greatest opera houses, from Leningrad to Buenos Aires, punctuated only by a skylight, an easel or two and a stove with a smoking stovepipe, but entirely filled up with the boisterous and sincere camaraderie of Rodolfo, Marcello, Colline, and their friends; a ripe, generous atmosphere into which Mimi is introduced like the first splinter of unavoidable death, and the scene melts imperceptibly into the terrace of the Café Momus, where the friends have gathered to drink and discuss philosophy, when suddenly the blond actress who had earlier been seen as Daffy Down Dilly returns as Musetta, mocking her elderly protector and pouring out peal after peal of deathless melody concerning the joys and advantages of life as a *grisette*, meanwhile clutching a small velvet handbag in which the contour of a small revolver was clearly visible, for as we well knew from previous experience, she was the symbol of the unexpectedness and exuberance of death, which we had waited to have come round again and which we would be meeting many times more during the course of the performance. There were murky scenes from television with a preponderance of excerpts from Jacques Cousteau documentaries with snorkeling figures disappearing down aqueous perspectives, past arrangements of coral still-lifes and white, fanlike creatures made of snowy tripe whose trailing vinelike tentacles could paralyze a man for life, and a seeming excess of silver bubbles constantly being emitted from here and there to sweep upward to the top of the screen, where they vanished. There were old clips from *Lucy*, *Lassie* and *The Waltons*; there was Walter Cronkite bidding us an urgent good evening years ago. Mostly there were just moments: a street corner viewed from above, bare branches flailing the sky, a child in a doorway, a painted Pennsylvania Dutch chest, a full moon disappearing behind a dark cloud to the accompaniment of a Japanese flute, a ballerina in a frosted white dress lifted up into the light.

Always behind it the circle in the sky remained fixed like a ghost on a television screen. The setting was now the last act of Ibsen's *When We Dead Awaken*: "A wild, broken mountaintop, with a sheer precipice behind. To the right tower snowy peaks, losing themselves high up in drifting mist. To the left, on a scree, stands on old, tumbledown hut. It is early morning. Dawn is breaking, the sun has not yet risen." Here the disc in the sky could begin to take on the properties of the sun that had been denied it for so long: as though made of wet wool, it began little by little to soak up and distribute light. The figure of Mercury had become both more theatrical and more human: no longer a statue, he was draped in a freshly laundered chlamys that set off his well-formed but slight physique; the broad-brimmed *petasus* sat charmingly on his curls. He sat, legs spread apart, on an iron park bench, digging absent-mindedly at the ground with his staff from which leaves rather than serpents sprouted, occasionally bending over to scratch the part of his heel behind the strap of his winged sandal. The morning mists were evaporating; the light was becoming the ordinary yellow daylight of the theater. Resting both hands on his staff, he leaned forward to address the audience, cocking his head in the shrewd bumpkin manner of a Will Rogers.

"So you think I have it, after all, or that I've found it? And you may be right. But I still say that what counts isn't the particular set of circumstances, but how we adapt ourselves to them, and you all must know that by now, watching all these changes of scene and scenery till you feel it's coming out of your ears. *I* know how it is; I've been everywhere, bearing messages to this one and that one, often steaming them open to see what's inside and getting a good dose of *that* too, in addition to the peaks of Tartarus which I might be flying over at the time. It's like sleeping too close to the edge of the bed—sometimes you're in danger of falling out on one side and sometimes on the other, but rarely do you fall out, and in general your dreams proceed pretty much in the normal way dreams have of proceeding. I still think the old plain way is better: the ideas, speeches, arguments—whatever you want to call 'em—on one hand, and strongly written scenes and fully fleshed-out characters in flannel suits and leg-o'-mutton sleeves on the other. For the new moon is most beautiful viewed through burnt twigs and the last few decrepit leaves still clinging to them."

Suddenly he glanced upward toward the scree and noticed a girl in a Victorian shirtwaist and a straw boater hat moving timidly down the path through the now wildly swirling mists. She was giggling silently with embarrassment and wonder, meanwhile clasping an old-fashioned kodak, which she had pointed at Mercury.

"It is Sabrina," he said. "The wheel has at last come full circle, and it is the simplicity of an encounter that was meant all along. It happened ever so many years ago, when we were children, and could have happened so many times since! But it isn't our fault that it has chosen this moment and this moment only, to repeat itself! For even if it does menace us directly, *it's exciting all the same!*"

And the avalanche fell and fell, and continues to fall even today.

THE PATH TO THE WHITE MOON

There were little farmhouses there they
Looked like farmhouses yes without very much land
And trees, too many trees and a mistake
Built into each thing rather charmingly
But once you have seen a thing you have to move on

You have to lie in the grass
And play with your hair, scratch yourself
And then the space of this behavior, the air,
Has suddenly doubled
And you have grown to fill the extra place
Looking back at the small, fallen shelter that was

If a stream winds through all this
Alongside an abandoned knitting mill it will not
Say where it has been
The time unfolds like music trapped on the page
Unable to tell the story again
Raging

Where the winters grew white we went outside
To look at things again, putting on more clothes
This too an attempt to define
How we were being in all the surroundings
Big ones sleepy ones
Underwear and hats speak to us
As though we were cats
Dependent and independent
There were shouted instructions
Grayed in the morning

Keep track of us
It gets to be so exciting but so big too

And we have ways to define but not the terms
Yet
We know what is coming, that we are moving
Dangerously and gracefully
Toward the resolution of time
Blurred but alive with many separate meanings
Inside this conversation

DITTO, KIDDO

How brave you are! *Sometimes.* And the injunction
Still stands, a plain white wall. More unfinished business.
But isn't that just the nature of business, someone else said, breezily.
You can't just pick up in the middle of it, and then leave off.
What if you do listen to it over and over, until

It becomes part of your soul, foreign matter that belongs there?
I ask you so many times to think about this rupture you are
Proceeding with, this revolution. And still time
Is draped around your shoulders. The weather report
Didn't mention rain, and you are ass-deep in it, so?
Find other predictions. These are good for throwing away,
Yesterday's newspapers, and those of the weeks before that spreading
Backward, away, almost in perfect order. It's all there
To interrupt your speaking. There is no other use to the past

Until those times when, driving abruptly off a road
Into a field you sit still and conjure the hours.
It was for this we made the small talk, the lies,
And whispered them over to give each the smell of truth,
But now, like biting devalued currency, they become possessions
As the stars come out. And the ridiculous machine
Still trickles mottoes: "Plastered again . . ." "from our house
To your house . . ." We wore these for a while, and they became us.

Each day seems full of itself, and yet it is only
A few colored beans and some straw lying on a dirt floor
In a mote-filled shaft of light. There *was* room. Yes,
And you have created it by going away. Somewhere, someone
Listens for your laugh, swallows it like a drink of cool water,
Neither happy nor aghast. And the stance, that post standing there,
  is you.

INTRODUCTION

To be a writer and write things
You must have experiences you can write about.
Just living won't do. I have a theory
About masterpieces, how to make them
At very little expense, and they're every
Bit as good as the others. You can
Use the same materials of the dream, at last.

It's a kind of game with no losers and only one
Winner—you. First, pain gets
Flashed back through the story and the story
Comes out backwards and woof-side up. This is
No one's story! At least they think that
For a time and the story is architecture
Now, and then history of a diversified kind.
A vacant episode during which the bricks got
Repointed and browner. And it ends up
Nobody's, there is nothing for any of us
Except that fretful vacillating around the central
Question that brings us closer,
For better and worse, for all this time.

I SEE, SAID THE BLIND MAN, AS HE PUT DOWN HIS HAMMER AND SAW

There is some charm in that old music
He'd fall for when the night wind released it—
Pleasant to be away; the stones fall back;
The hill of gloom in place over the roar
Of the kitchens but with remembrance like a bright patch
Of red in a bunch of laundry. But will the car
Ever pull away and spunky at all times he'd
Got the mission between the ladder
And the slices of bread someone had squirted astrology over
Until it took the form of a man, obtuse, out of pocket
Perhaps, probably standing there.

Can't you see how we need these far-from-restful pauses?
And in the wind neighbors and such agree
It's a hard thing, a milestone of sorts in some way?
So that the curtains contribute what charm they can
To the spectacle: an overflowing cesspool
Among the memoirs of court life, the candy, cigarettes,
And what else. What kind is it, is there more than one
Kind, are people forever going to be at the edge
Of things, even the nice ones, and when it happens
Will we all be alone together? The armor
Of these thoughts laughs at itself
Yet the distances are always growing
With everything between, in between.

EDITION PETERS, LEIPZIG

Another blueprint: some foxing, woolly the foliage
On this dusky shrine
Under the glass dome on the spinet
To make it seem all these voices were once one.
Outside, the rout continues:
The clash erupting to the very door, but the
Door is secure. There is room here still
For thoughts like ferns being integrated
Into another system, something to scare the night away,
And when morning comes they have gone, only the dew
Remains. What more did we want anyway?
I'm sorry. We believe there is something more than attributes
And coefficients, that the giant erection
Is something more than the peg on which our lives hang,
Ours, yours . . . The core is not concern
But for afternoon busy with blinds open, restless with
Search-and-destroy missions, the approach to business is new
And ancient and mellow at the same time. For them to gain
Their end, the peace of fireworks on a vanishing sky,
We have to bother. Please welcome the three insane interviewers
Each with his astrolabe and question.
And the days drain into the sea.

37 HAIKU

Old-fashioned shadows hanging down, that difficulty in love too soon

Some star or other went out, and you, thank you for your book
and year

Something happened in the garage and I owe it for the blood traffic

Too low for nettles but it is exactly the way people think and feel

And I think there's going to be even more but waist-high

Night occurs dimmer each time with the pieces of light smaller and
squarer

You have original artworks hanging on the walls oh I said edit

You nearly undermined the brush I now place against the ball field
arguing

That love was a round place and will still be there two years
from now

And it is a dream sailing in a dark unprotected cove

Pirates imitate the ways of ordinary people myself for instance

Planted over and over that land has a bitter aftertaste

A blue anchor grains of grit in a tall sky sewing

He is a monster like everyone else but what do you do if you're
a monster

Like him feeling him come from far away and then go down to
his car

The wedding was enchanted everyone was glad to be in it

What trees, tools, why ponder socks on the premises

Come to the edge of the barn the property really begins there

In a smaller tower shuttered and put away there

You lay aside your hair like a book that is too important to read now

Why did witches pursue the beast from the eight sides of the country

A pencil on glass—shattered! The water runs down the drain

In winter sometimes you see those things and also in summer

A child must go down it must stand and last

Too late the last express passes through the dust of gardens

A vest—there is so much to tell about even in the side rooms

Hesitantly, it built up and passed quickly without unlocking

There are some places kept from the others and are separate, they
never exist

I lost my ridiculous accent without acquiring another

In Buffalo, Buffalo she was praying, the nights stick together like
pages in an old book

The dreams descend like cranes on gilded, forgetful wings

What is the past, what is it all for? A mental sandwich?

Did you say, hearing the schooner overhead, we turned back to
the weir?

In rags and crystals, sometimes with a shred of sense, an odd dignity

The boy must have known the particles fell through the house
after him

All in all we were taking our time, the sea returned—no more pirates

I inch and only sometimes as far as the twisted pole gone in
spare colors

HAIBUN

Wanting to write something I could think only of my own ideas, though you surely have your separate, private being in some place I will never walk through. And then of the dismal space between us, filled though it may be with interesting objects, standing around like trees waiting to be discovered. It may be that this is the intellectual world. But if so, what poverty—even the discoveries yet to be made, and which shall surprise us, even us. It must be heightened somehow, but not to brutality. That is an invention and not a true instinct, and this must never be invented. Yet I am forced to invent, even if during the process I become a *songe-creux*, inaccurate dreamer, and these inventions are then to be claimed by the first person who happens on them. I'm hoping that homosexuals not yet born get to inquire about it, inspect the whole random collection as though it were a sphere. Isn't the point of pain the possibility it brings of being able to get along without pain, for awhile, of manipulating our marionette-like limbs in the straitjacket of air, and so to have written something? Unprofitable shifts of light and dark in the winter sky address this dilemma very directly. In time to come we shall perceive them as the rumpled linen or scenery through which we did walk once, for a short time, during some sort of vacation. It is a frostbitten, brittle world but once you are inside it you want to stay there always.

The year—not yet abandoned but a living husk, a lesson

HAIBUN 2

. . . and can see the many hidden ways merit drains out of the established and internationally acclaimed containers, like a dry patch of sky. It is an affair of some enormity. The sky is swathed in a rich, gloomy and finally silly grandeur, like drapery in a portrait by Lebrun. This is to indicate that our actions in this tiny, tragic platform are going to be more than usually infinitesimal, given the superhuman scale on which we have to operate, and also that we should not take any comfort from the inanity of our situation; we are still valid creatures with a job to perform, and the arena facing us, though titanic, hasn't rolled itself beyond the notion of dimension. It isn't suitable, and it's here. Shadows are thrown out at the base of things at right angles to the regular shadows that are already there, pointing in the correct direction. They are faint but not invisible, and it seems appropriate to start intoning the litany of dimensions there, at the base of a sapling spreading its lines in two directions. The temperature hardens, and things like the smell and the mood of water are suddenly more acute, and may help us. We will never know whether they did.

Water, a bossa nova, a cello is centred, the light behind the library

HAIBUN 3

I was swimming with the water at my back, funny thing is it was real this time. I mean this time it was working. We weren't too far from shore, the guides hadn't noticed yet. Always you work out of the possibility of being injured, but this time, all the new construction, the new humiliation, you have to see it. Guess it's OK to take a look. But a cup of tea—you wouldn't want to spill it. And a grapefruit (spelled "grapfruit" on the small, painstakingly lettered card) after a while, and the new gray suit. Then more, and more, it was a kind of foliage or some built-in device to trip you. Make you fall. The encounter with the silence of permissiveness stretching away like a moonlit sea to the horizon, whatever that really is. *They* want you to like it. And you honor them in liking it. You cause pleasure before sleep insists, draws over to where you may yet be. And some believe this is merely a detail. And they may be right. And we may be the whole of which all that truly happens is only peelings and shreds of bark. Not that we are too much more than these. Remember they don't have to thank you for it either.

The subtracted sun, all I'm going by here, with the boy, this new maneuver is less than the letter in the wind

HAIBUN 4

Dark at four again. Sadly I negotiate the almost identical streets as little by little they are obliterated under a rain of drips and squiggles of light. Their message of universal brotherhood through suffering is taken from the top, the pedal held down so that the first note echoes throughout the piece without becoming exactly audible. It collects over different parts of the city and the drift in those designated parts is different from elsewhere. It is a man, it was one all along. No it isn't. It is a man with the conscience of a woman, always coming out of something, turning to look at you, wondering about a possible reward. How sweet to my sorrow is this man's knowledge in his way of coming, the brotherhood that will surely result under now darkened skies.

The pressing, pressing urgent whispers, pushing on, seeing directly

HAIBUN 5

Bring them all back to life, with white gloves on, out of the dream in which they are still alive. Loosen the adhesive bonds that tie them to the stereotypes of the dead, clichés like the sound of running water. Abruptly it was winter again. A slope several football fields wide sprang out of the invisible foreground, the one behind me, and unlaced its barren provocation upwards, with flair and menace, at a 20-degree angle—the ascending night and also the voice in it that means to be heard, a pagoda of which is visible at the left horizon, not meaning much: the flurry of a cold wind. We're in it too chortled the rowanberries. And how fast so much aggressiveness unfolded, like a swiftly flowing, silent stream. Along its banks world history presented itself as a series of translucent tableaux, fading imperceptibly into one another, so that the taking of Quebec by the British in 1629 melts into the lollipop tints of Marquette and Joliet crossing the mouth of the Missouri River. But at the center a rope of distress twists itself ever tighter around some of the possessions we brought from the old place and were going to arrange here. And what about the courteous but dispassionate gaze of an armed messenger on his way from someplace to someplace else that is the speech of all the old, resurrected loves, tinged with respect, caring to see that you are no longer alone now in this dream you chose. The dark yellowish flow of light drains out of the slanted dish of the sky and from the masses of the loved a tremendous chant arises: We are viable! And so back into the city with its glimmers of possibility like Broadway nights of notoriety and the warm syrup of embarrassed and insistent proclamations of all kinds of tidings that made you what you were in the world and made the world for you, only diminished once it had been seen and become the object of further speculation leading like railroad ties out of the present inconclusive sphere into the world of two dimensions.

A terminus, pole fringed with seaweed at its base, a cracked memory

HAIBUN 6

To be involved in every phase of directing, acting, producing and so on must be infinitely rewarding. Just as when a large, fat, lazy frog hops off his lily pad like a spitball propelled by a rubber band and disappears into the water of the pond with an enthusiastic plop. It cannot be either changed or improved on. So too with many of life's little less-than-pleasurable experiences, like the rain that falls and falls for so long that no one can remember when it began or what weather used to be, or cares much either; they are much too busy trying to plug holes in ceilings or emptying pails and other containers and then quickly pushing them back to catch the overflow. But nobody seems eager to accord ideal status to this situation and I, for one, would love to know why. Don't we realize that after all these centuries that are now starting to come apart like moldy encyclopedias in some abandoned, dusty archive that we have to take the bitter with the sweet or soon all distinctions will be submerged by the tide of tepid approval of everything that is beginning to gather force and direction as well? And when its mighty roar threatens in earnest the partially submerged bridges and cottages, picks up the floundering cattle to deposit them in trees and so on to who knows what truly horrible mischief, it will be time, then, to genuinely rethink this and come up with true standards of evaluation, only it will be too late of course, too late for anything but the satisfaction that lasts only just so long. A pity, though. Meanwhile I lift my glass to these black-and-silver striped nights. I believe that the rain never drowned sweeter, more prosaic things than those we have here, now, and I believe this is going to have to be enough.

Striped hair, inquisitive gloves, a face, some woman named Ernestine Throckmorton, white opera glasses and more

VARIATION ON A NOEL

" . . . when the snow lay round about,
deep and crisp and even . . ."

A year away from the pigpen, and look at him.
A thirsty unit by an upending stream,
Man doctors, God supplies the necessary medication
If elixir were to be found in the world's dolor, where is none.

A thirsty unit by an upending stream,
Ashamed of the moon, of everything that hides too little of her
nakedness—
If elixir were to be found in the world's dolor, where is none,
Out emancipation should be great and steady.

Ashamed of the moon, of everything that hides too little of her
nakedness,
The twilight prayers begin to emerge on a country crossroads.
Our emancipation should be great and steady
As crossword puzzles done in this room, this after-effect.

The twilight prayers begin to emerge on a country crossroads
Where no sea contends with the interest of the cherry trees.
As crossword puzzles done in this room, this after-effect,
I see the whole thing written down.

Where no sea contends with the interest of the cherry trees
Everything but love was abolished. It stayed on, a stepchild.
I see the whole thing written down:
Business, a lack of drama. Whatever the partygoing public needs.

Everything but love was abolished. It stayed on, a stepchild.
The bent towers of the playroom advanced to something like
openness,
Business, a lack of drama. Whatever the partygoing public needs
To be kind, and to forget, passing through the next doors.

The bent towers of the playroom advanced to something like
openness.
But if you heard it, and you didn't want it
To be kind, and to forget, passing through the next doors
(For we believe him not exiled from the skies) . . .

But if you heard it, and if you didn't want it,
Why do I call to you after all this time?
For we believe him not exiled from the skies.
Because I wish to give only what the specialist can give,

Why do I call to you after all this time?
Your own friends, running for mayor, behaving outlandishly
Because I wish to give only what the specialist can give,
Spend what they care to.

Your own friends, running for mayor, behaving outlandishly,
(And I have known him cheaply)
Spend what they care to.
A form of ignorance, you might say. Let's leave that though.

And I have known him cheaply.
Agree to remove all that concern, another exodus—
A form of ignorance, you might say. Let's leave that though.
The mere whiteness was a blessing, taking us far.

Agree to remove all that concern, another exodus.
A year away from the pigpen, and look at him.
The mere whiteness was a blessing, taking us far.
Man doctors, God supplies the necessary medication.

STAFFAGE

Sir, I am one of a new breed
Of inquisitive pest in love with the idea
Of our integrity, programming us over dark seas
Into small offices, where we sit and compete
With you, on your own time.
We want only to be recognized for what we are;
Everything else is secondary.
Consequently, I shall sit on your doorstep
Till you notice me. I'm still too young
To be overlooked, yet not old enough to qualify
For full attention. I'll flesh out
The thin warp of your dreams, make them meatier,
Nuttier. And when a thin pall gathers,
Leading finally to outraged investigation
Into what matters next, I'll be there
On the other side.
                                        Half of me I give
To do with as you wish—scold, ignore, forget for awhile.
The other half I keep, and shall feel
Fully rewarded if you pass by this offer
Without recognizing it, receding deliberately
Into the near distance, which speaks no longer
Of loss, but of brevity rather: short naps, keeping fit.

THE LONEDALE OPERATOR

The first movie I ever saw was the Walt Disney cartoon *The Three Little Pigs*. My grandmother took me to it. It was back in the days when you went "downtown." There was a second feature, with live actors, called *Bring 'Em Back Alive*, a documentary about the explorer Frank Buck. In this film you saw a python swallow a live pig. This wasn't scary. In fact, it seemed quite normal, the sort of thing you *would* see in a movie—"reality."

A little later we went downtown again to see a movie of *Alice in Wonderland*, also with live actors. This wasn't very surprising either. I think I knew something about the story; maybe it had been read to me. That wasn't why it wasn't surprising, though. The reason was that these famous movie actors, like W. C. Fields and Gary Cooper, were playing different roles, and even though I didn't know who they were, they were obviously important for doing other kinds of acting, and so it didn't seem strange that they should be acting in a special way like this, pretending to be characters that people already knew about from a book. In other words, I imagined specialties for them just from having seen this one example. And I was right, too, though not about the film, which I liked. Years later I saw it when I was grown up and thought it was awful. How could I have been wrong the first time? I knew it wasn't inexperience, because somehow I was experienced the first time I saw a movie. It was as though my taste had changed, though I had not, and I still can't help feeling that I was right the first time, when I was still relatively unencumbered by my experience.

I forget what were the next movies I saw and will skip ahead to one I saw when I was grown up, *The Lonedale Operator*, a silent short by D. W. Griffith, made in 1911 and starring Blanche Sweet. Although I was in my twenties when I saw it at the Museum of Modern Art, it seems as remote from me in time as my first viewing of *Alice in Wonderland*. I can remember almost none of it, and the little I can remember may have been in another Griffith short, *The*

Lonely Villa, which may have been on the same program. It seems that Blanche Sweet was a heroic telephone operator who managed to get through to the police and foil some gangsters who were trying to rob a railroad depot, though I also see this living room —small, though it was supposed to be in a large house—with Mary Pickford running around, and this may have been a scene in *The Lonely Villa*. At that moment the memories stop, and terror, or tedium, sets in. It's hard to tell which is which in this memory, because the boredom of living in a lonely place or having a lonely job, and even of being so far in the past and having to wear those funny uncomfortable clothes and hairstyles is terrifying, more so than the intentional scariness of the plot, the criminals, whoever they were.

Imagine that innocence (Lilian Harvey) encounters romance (Willy Fritsch) in the home of experience (Albert Basserman). From there it is only a step to terror, under the dripping boughs outside. Anything can change as fast as it wants to, and in doing so may pass through a more or less terrible phase, but the true terror is in the swiftness of changing, forward or backward, slipping always just beyond our control. The actors are like people on drugs, though they aren't doing anything unusual—as a matter of fact, they are performing brilliantly.

PROUST'S QUESTIONNAIRE

I am beginning to wonder
Whether this alternative to
Sitting back and doing something quiet
Is the clever initiative it seemed. It's
Also relaxation and sunlight branching into
Passionate melancholy, jealousy of something unknown;
And our minds, parked in the sky over New York,
Are nonetheless responsible. Nights
When the paper comes
And you walk around the block
Wrenching yourself from the lover every five minutes
And it hurts, yet nothing is ever really clean
Or two-faced. You are losing your grip
And there are still flowers and compliments in the air:
"How did you like the last one?"
"Was I good?" "I think it stinks."

It's a question of questions, first:
The nuts-and-bolts kind you know you can answer
And the impersonal ones you answer almost without meaning to:
"My greatest regret." "What keeps the world from falling down."
And then the results are brilliant:
Someone is summoned to a name, and soon
A roomful of people becomes dense and contoured
And words come out of the wall
To batter the rhythm of generation following on generation.

And I see once more how everything
Must be up to me: here a calamity to be smoothed away
Like ringlets, there the luck of uncoding
This singular cipher of primary
And secondary colors, and the animals
With us in the ark, happy to be there as it settles
Into an always more violent sea.

CUPS WITH BROKEN HANDLES

So much variation
In what is basically a one-horse town:
Part of me frivolous, part intentionally crude,
And part unintentionally thoughtless.
Modesty and false modesty stroll hand in hand
Like twin girls. But there are more abstract things too
That play a larger role. The intense, staccato repetitions
Of whatever. You don't know and we don't know either.

From there it's a big, though necessary, leap to
The more subtly conceptual conditionings: your opinion
Of you shaped in the vacuum-form of suppositions,
Correct or false, of others, and how we can never be ourselves
While so much of us is going on in the minds of other people,
People you meet on the street who greet you strangely
As though remembering a recent trip to the Bahamas
And say things like: "It is broken. But we'd heard
You heard too. Isn't it too bad about old things, old schools,
Old dishes, with nothing to do but sit and wait
Their turn. Meanwhile you're
Looking stretched again, concentrated, as you do not pass
From point A to point B but merely speculate
On how it would be, and in that instant
Do appear to be traveling, though we all
Stay home, don't we. Our strength lies
In the potential for motion, not in accomplishments, and it gets
Used up too, which is, in a way, more effective."

JUST SOMEONE YOU SAY HI TO

But what about me, I
Wondered as the parachute released
Its carrousel into the sky over me?
I never think about it
Unless I think about it all the time
And therefore don't know except in dreams
How I behave, what I mean to myself.
Should I wonder more
How I'm doing, inquire more after you
With the face like a birthday present
I am unwrapping as the parachute wanders
Through us, across blue ridges brown with autumn leaves?

People are funny—they see it
And then it's that that they want.
No wonder we look out from ourselves
To the other person going on.
What about my end of the stick?
I keep thinking if I could get through you
I'd get back to me at a further stage
Of this journey, but the tent flaps fall,
The parachute won't land, only drift sideways.
The carnival never ends; the apples,
The land, are duly tucked away
And we are left with only sensations of ourselves
And the dry otherness, like a clenched fist
Around the throttle as we go down, sideways and down.

THEY LIKE

They like to drink beer and wave their hands and whistle
Much as human beings everywhere do. Dark objects loom
Out of the night, attracted by the light of conversations,
And they take note of that, thinking how funny everything is.

It was a long time ago that you began. The dawn was brittle
And open, and things stayed in it for a long time as images
After the projecting urge had left. In the third year a tension
Arose like smoke on the horizon, but it was quickly subdued.
And now in the fifth year you return with tears
That are, I understand, a formality, to seal the naked time
And pave it over so that it may be walked across. The day with
Its straw flowers and dried fruits is for "putting up" too.

At a corner you meet the one who makes you glad, like a stranger
Off on some business. Come again soon. I will,
I will. Only this time let your serious proposals stick out
Into the bay a considerable distance, like piers. Remember
I am not the stranger I seem to be, only casual
And ruthless, but kind. Kind and strange. It isn't a warning.

The flares in the lower sky are no longer ambitious
But a steady, droning red. That's my middle initial up there,
Hanging over a populous city. Flowers and fires everywhere,
A warning surely. But they all lead their lives appropriately
Into desperation, and nobody seems surprised. Only the story
Stays behind, when they go away, sitting on a stone. It grew
and grew.

SO MANY LIVES

Sometimes I get radiant drunk when I think of and/or look at you,
Upstaged by our life, with me in it.
And other mornings too
Your care is like a city, with the uncomfortable parts
Evasive, and difficult to connect with the plan
That was, and the green diagonals of the rain kind of
Fudging to rapidly involve everything that stood out,
And doing so in an illegal way, but it doesn't matter,
It's rapture that counts, and what little
There is of it is seldom aboveboard,
That's its nature,
What we take our cue from.
It masquerades as worry, first, then as self-possession
In which I am numb, imagining I am this vision
Of ships stuck on the tarpaper of an urban main,
At night, coal stars glinting,
And you the ruby lights hung far above on pylons,
Seeming to own the night and the nearer reaches
Of a civilization we feel as ours,
The lining of our old doing.

I can walk away from you
Because I know I can always call, and in the end we will
Be irresolutely joined,
Laughing over this alphabet of connivance
That never goes on too long, because outside
My city there is wind, and burning straw and other things that
   don't coincide,
To which we'll be condemned, perhaps, some day.
Now our peace is in our assurance
And has that savor,
Its own blind deduction
Of whatever would become of us if

We were alone, to nurture on this shore some fable
To block out that other whose remote being
Becomes every day a little more sentient and more suavely realized.
I'll believe it when the police pay *you* off.
In the meantime there are so many things not to believe in
We can make a hobby of them, as long as we continue to uphold
The principle of private property.
So what if ours is planted with tin-can trees
It's better than a forest full of parked cars with the lights out,
Because the effort of staying back to side with someone
For whom number is everything
Will finally unplug the dark
And the black acacias stand out as symbols, lovers
Of what men will at last stop doing to each other
When we can be quiet, and start counting sheep to stay awake
together.

NEVER SEEK TO TELL THY LOVE

Many colors will take you to themselves
But now I want someone to tell me how to get home.
The way back there is streaked and stippled,
A shaded place. It belongs where it is going

Not where it is. The flowers don't talk to Ida now.
They speak only the language of flowers,
Saying things like, How hard I tried to get there.
It must mean I'm not here yet. But you,
You seem so formal, so serious. You can't read poetry,
Not the way they taught us back in school.

Returning to the point was always the main thing, then.
Did we ever leave it? I don't think so. It was our North Pole.
We skulked and hungered there for years, and now,
Like dazzled insects skimming the bright airs,
You are back on the road again, the path leading
Vigorously upward, through intelligent and clear spaces.
They don't make rocks like us any more.

And holding on to the thread, fine as a cobweb, but incredibly strong,
Each of us advances into his own labyrinth.
The gift of invisibility
Has been granted to all but the gods, so we say such things,
Filling the road up with colors, faces,
Tender speeches, until they feed us to the truth.

DARLENE'S HOSPITAL

The hospital: it wasn't her idea
That the colors should slide muddy from the brush
And spew their random evocations everywhere,
Provided that things should pick up next season.
It was a way of living, to her way of thinking.
She took a job, it wasn't odd.
But then, backing through the way many minds had been made up,
It came again, the color, always a color
Climbing the apple of the sky, often
A secret lavender place you weren't supposed to look into.
And then a sneeze would come along
Or soon we'd be too far out from shore, on a milky afternoon
Somewhere in late August with the paint flaking off,
The lines of traffic flowing like mucus.
And they won't understand its importance, it's too bad,
Not even when it's too late.

Now we're often happy. The dark car
Moves heftily away along low bluffs,
And if we don't have our feelings, what
Good are we, but whose business is it?
Beware the happy man: once she perched light
In the reading space of my room, a present joy
For all time to come, whatever happens;
And still we rotate, gathering speed until
Nothing is there but more speed in the light ahead.
Such moments as we prized in life:
The promise of a new day, living with lots of people
All headed in more or less the same direction, the sound of this
In the embracing stillness, but not the brutality,
And lists of examples of lots of things, and shit—
What more could we conceivably be satisfied with, it is
Joy, and undaunted

She leaves the earth at that point,
Intersecting all our daydreams of breakfast and lunch.
The Lady of Shalott's in hot water again.

This and the dreams of any of the young
Were not her care. The river flowed
Hard by the hospital from whose gilded
Balconies and turrets fair spirits waved,
Lonely, like us. Here be no pursuers,
Only imagined animals and cries
In the wilderness, which made it "the wilderness,"
And suddenly the lonesomeness becomes a pleasant city
Fanning out around a lake; you get to meet
Precisely the person who would have been here now,
A dream no longer, and are polished and directed
By his deliberate grasp, back
To the reality that was always there despairing
Of your return as months and years went by,
Now silent again forever, the perfect space,
Attuned to your wristwatch
As though time would never go away again.

His dirty mind
Produced it all, an oratorio based on love letters
About our sexual habits in the early 1950s.
It wasn't that these stories weren't true,
Only that a different kind of work
Of the imagination had grown up around them, taller
Than redwoods, and not
Wanting to embarrass them, effaced itself
To the extent that a colossus could, and so you looked
And saw nothing, but suddenly felt better
Without wondering why. And the serial continues:

Pain, expiation, delight, more pain,
A frieze that lengthens continually, in the happy way
Friezes do, and no plot is produced,
Nothing you could hang an identifying question on.
It's an imitation of pleasure; it may not work
But at least we'll know then that we'll have done
What we could, and chalk it up to virtue
Or just plain laziness. And if she glides
Backwards through us, a finger hooked
Out of death, we shall not know where the mystery began:
Inaccurate dreamers of our state,
Sodden from sitting in the rain too long.

DESTINY WALTZ

Everyone has some work to be done
And after that they may have some fun.
Which sometimes leads to distraction.
Older faces than yours

Have been whirled away on heaven
Knows what wind like painted leaves in autumn.
Seriousness doesn't help either:
Just when you get on it it slips its tether,
Laughing, runs happily away.

It is a question of forbearance among the days.
Ask, but not too often: that way most ways
Of leading up to the truth will approach you
Timidly at first, wanting to get to know you
Before wandering away on other paths
Leading out of your meanwhile safe precinct.
Your feet know what they're doing.

And if later in the year some true fear,
A real demon comes to be installed
In the sang-froid of not doing anything,
The shoe is on the other foot
This time,
Just this one time.

Romance removes so much of this
Yet staying behind while it does so
Is no way to agitate
To break the year's commotion where it loomed
Sharpest and most full. It's a trance.

TRY ME!
I'M DIFFERENT!

Obviously the guts and beauty are going to be denied again
This time around, as we all meet at twilight
In a level place surrounded by tall trees. It's another kind of contest.
Whatever is sworn, promised, sealed
With kisses, over and over, is as strange, faithless
And fundamentally unlike us as the ocean when it fills
Deep crevices far inland, more deeply involved with the land
Than anyone suspected. Such are our games,

And so also the way we thought of them
In the time behind the telling. Now it goes smoothly
Under glass. The contours and color contrasts are
Sharper, but there is no sound. And I didn't deliberately
Try to hide my ambition, wearing the same tweed jacket
For the fourteenth season; instead I thought its pedigree something
To notice. But the question of style has been
Turned inside out in the towns where we never meet.

I lived so long without being scolded that I grew
To feel I was beyond criticism, until I flew
Those few paces from the nest. Now, I understand,
My privilege means giving up all claims on life
As the casual, criminal thing it sometimes is, in favor of
A horizon in whose cursive recesses we
May sometimes lie concealed because we are part
Of the pattern. No one misses you. The future

Ignores those streaming with a present so heavy
And intense we are subdued by the outline.
No one criticizes us for lacking depth,
But the scandal shimmers, around and elsewhere.
If we could finally pry open the gate to the pastures of the times,
No sickness would be evident. And the colors we adduced
Would supply us, parables ourselves, told in our own words.

ONE OF THE MOST EXTRAORDINARY THINGS IN LIFE

must never be *invented.* It shall have been.
Once its umbrella of truth is raised to become
And tall trees follow it as though it were Orpheus,
Its music, in trouble, slows down to a complete standstill,

Still in trouble, but has become a cube
With all the outside faces reflecting
What we did before we got here. One of us,
A little poorer than the others, half-turns

To divulge a truth in low relief that another
Messenger would have been killed for: it isn't
Our waiting that makes us worthy of having been here forever,
Only the wild groves you read about, that no one

Has probably ever seen. I hear they have caves
In which men as old as the earth live, that when
These die, nothing ever takes their place.
Therefore, why weep we, mourners, around

A common block of space?

WHATEVER IT IS, WHEREVER YOU ARE

The cross-hatching technique which allowed our ancestors to exchange certain genetic traits for others, in order to provide their offspring with a way of life at once more variegated and more secure than their own, has just about run out of steam and has left us wondering, once more, what there is about this plush solitude that makes us think we will ever get out, or even want to. The ebony hands of the clock always seem to mark the same hour. That is why it always seems the same, though it is of course changing constantly, subtly, as though fed by an underground stream. If only we could go out in back, as when we were kids, and smoke and fool around and just stay out of the way, for a little while. But that's just it—don't you see? We are "out in back." No one has ever used the front door. We have always lived in this place without a name, without shame, a place for grownups to talk and laugh, having a good time. When we were children it seemed that adulthood would be like climbing a tree, that there would be a view from there, breathtaking because slightly more elusive. But now we can see only down, first down through the branches and further down the surprisingly steep grass patch that slopes away from the base of the tree. It certainly is a different view, but not the one we expected.

What did *they* want us to do? Stand around this way, monitoring every breath, checking each impulse for the return address, wondering constantly about evil until necessarily we fall into a state of torpor that is probably the worst sin of all? To what purpose did they cross-hatch so effectively, so that the luminous surface that was underneath is transformed into another, also luminous but so shifting and so alive with suggestiveness that it is like quicksand, to take a step there would be to fall through the fragile net of uncertainties into the bog of certainty, otherwise known as the Slough of Despond?

Probably they meant for us to enjoy the things they enjoyed, like late summer evenings, and hoped that we'd find others and thank them for providing us with the wherewithal to find and enjoy them. Singing the way they did, in the old time, we can sometimes see through the tissues and tracings the genetic process has laid down between us and them. The tendrils can suggest a hand, or a specific color—the yellow of the tulip, for instance—will flash for a moment in such a way that after it has been withdrawn we can be sure that there was no imagining, no auto-suggestion here, but at the same time it becomes as useless as all subtracted memories. It has brought certainty without heat or light. Yet still in the old time, in the faraway summer evenings, they must have had a word for this, or known that we would someday need one, and wished to help. Then it is that a kind of purring occurs, like the wind sneaking around the baseboards of a room: not the infamous "still, small voice" but an ancillary speech that is parallel to the slithering of our own doubt-fleshed imaginings, a visible soundtrack of the way we sound as we move from encouragement to despair to exasperation and back again, with a gesture sometimes that is like an aborted movement outward toward some cape or promontory from which the view would extend in two directions—backward and forward—but that is only a polite hope in the same vein as all the others, crumpled and put away, and almost not to be distinguished from any of them, except that *it knows we know*, and in the context of not knowing is a fluidity that flashes like silver, that seems to say a film has been exposed and an image will, most certainly will, not like the last time, come to consider itself within the frame.

It must be an old photograph of you, out in the yard, looking almost afraid in the crisp, raking light that afternoons in the city held in those days, unappeased, not accepting anything from anybody. So what else is new? I'll tell you what is: you are accepting this now from the invisible, unknown sender, and the light that was intended, you thought, only to rake or glance is now directed full in your face, as it in fact always was, but you were squinting so hard, fearful of accepting it, that you didn't know this. Whether it warms or burns is another matter, which we will not go into here. The point is that you are accepting it and holding on to it, like love from someone you always thought you couldn't stand, and whom you now recognize as a brother, an equal. Someone whose face is the same as yours in the photograph but who is someone else, all of whose thoughts and feelings are directed at you, falling like a gentle slab of light that will ultimately loosen and dissolve the crusted suspicion, the timely self-hatred, the efficient cold directness, the horrible good manners, the sensible resolves and the senseless nights spent waiting in utter abandon, that have grown up to be you in the tree with no view; and place you firmly in the good-natured circle of your ancestors' games and entertainments.

TREFOIL

Imagine some tinkling curiosity from the years back—
The fashions aren't old enough yet to look out of fashion.
It is a picture of patient windows, with trees
Of two minds half-caught in their buzz and luster,
The froth of everyone's ideas as personal and skimpy as ever.

The windows taught us one thing: a great, square grief
Not alleviated or distracted by anything, since the pattern
Must establish itself before it can grow old, cannot weather nicely
Keeping a notion of squirrels and peacocks to punctuate
Chapters of fine print as they are ground down, growing ever finer
To assume the strict title of dust someday. No, there is no room now
For oceans, blizzards: only night, with fingers of steel
Pressing the lost lid, searching forever unquietly the mechanism
To unclasp all this into warbled sunlight, the day
The gaunt parson comes to ask for your hand. Nothing is flying,
Sinking; it is as though the resistance of all things
To the earth were so much casual embroidery, years
In the making, barely glimpsed at the appointed time.

Through it all a stiffness persists
Of someone who had changed her mind, moved by your arguments
And waiting till the last possible moment to confess it,
To let you know you were wanted, even a lot, more than you could
Imagine. But all that is, as they say, another story.

PROBLEMS

Rough stares, sometimes a hello,
A something to carry. Yes and over it
The feeling of one to one like leaves blowing
Between this imaginary, real world and the sky
Which is sometimes a terrible color
But is surely always and only as we imagine it?
I forgot to say there are extra things.
Once, someone—my father—came to me and spoke
Extreme words amid the caution of the time.
I was too drunk, too scared to know what was being said
Around us then, only that it was a final
Shelving off, that it was now and never,
The way things would come to pass.
You can subscribe to this.
It always lets you know how well
You're doing, how well along the thing is with its growing.
Was it a pattern of wheat
On the spotted walls you wanted to show me
Or are these the things always coming,
The churning, moving support that lets us rock still?

A WAVE

To pass through pain and not know it,
A car door slamming in the night.
To emerge on an invisible terrain.

So the luck of speaking out
A little too late came to be worshipped in various guises:
A mute actor, a future saint intoxicated with the idea of martyrdom;
And our landscape came to be as it is today:
Partially out of focus, some of it too near, the middle distance
A haven of serenity and unreachable, with all kinds of nice
People and plants waking and stretching, calling
Attention to themselves with every artifice of which the human
Genre is capable. And they called it our home.

No one came to take advantage of these early
Reverses, no doorbell rang;
Yet each day of the week, once it had arrived, seemed the threshold
Of love and desperation again. At night it sang
In the black trees: *My mindless, oh my mindless, oh.*
And it could be that it was Tuesday, with dark, restless clouds
And puffs of white smoke against them, and below, the wet streets
That seem so permanent, and all of a sudden the scene changes:
It's another idea, a new conception, something submitted
A long time ago, that only now seems about to work
To destroy at last the ancient network
Of letters, diaries, ads for civilization.
It passes through you, emerges on the other side
And is now a distant city, with all
The possibilities shrouded in a narrative moratorium.
The chroniqueurs who bad-mouthed it, the honest
Citizens whose going down into the day it was,
Are part of it, though none

Stand with you as you mope and thrash your way through time,
Imagining it as it is, a kind of tragic euphoria
In which your spirit sprouted. And which is justified in you.

In the haunted house no quarter is given: in that respect
It's very much business as usual. The reductive principle
Is no longer there, or isn't enforced as much as before.
There will be no getting away from the prospector's
Hunch; past experience matters again; the tale will stretch on
For miles before it is done. There would be more concerts
From now on, and the ground on which a man and his wife could
Look at each other and laugh, remembering how love is to them,
Shrank and promoted a surreal intimacy, like jazz music
Moving over furniture, to say how pleased it was
Or something. In the end only a handshake
Remains, something like a kiss, but fainter. Were we
Making sense? Well, that thirst will account for some
But not all of the marvelous graffiti; meanwhile
The oxygen of the days sketches the rest,
The balance. Our story is no longer alone.
There is a rumbling there
And now it ends, and in a luxurious hermitage
The straws of self-defeat are drawn. The short one wins.

One idea is enough to organize a life and project it
Into unusual but viable forms, but many ideas merely
Lead one thither into a morass of their own good intentions.
Think how many the average person has during the course of a day,
   or night,
So that they become a luminous backdrop to ever-repeated
Gestures, having no life of their own, but only echoing
The suspicions of their possessor. It's fun to scratch around

And maybe come up with something. But for the tender blur
Of the setting to mean something, words must be ejected bodily,
A certain crispness be avoided in favor of a density
Of strutted opinion doomed to wilt in oblivion: not too linear
Nor yet too puffed and remote. Then the advantage of
Sinking in oneself, crashing through the skylight of one's own
Received opinions redirects the maze, setting up significant
Erections of its own at chosen corners, like gibbets,
And through this the mesmerizing plan of the landscape becomes,
At last, apparent. It is no more a landscape than a golf course is,
Though sensibly a few natural bonuses have been left in. And as it
Focuses itself, it is the backward part of a life that is
Partially coming into view. It's there, like a limb. And the issue
Of making sense becomes such a far-off one. Isn't this "sense"—
This little of my life that I can see, that answers me
Like a dog, and wags its tail, though excitement and fidelity are
About all that ever gets expressed? What did I ever do
To want to wander over into something else, an explanation
Of how I behaved, for instance, when knowing can have this
Sublime rind of excitement, like the shore of a lake in the desert
Blazing with the sunset? So that if it pleases all my constructions
To collapse, I shall at least have had that satisfaction, and known
That it need not be permanent in order to stay alive,
Beaming, confounding with the spell of its good manners.

As with rocks at low tide, a mixed surface is revealed,
More detritus. Still, it is better this way
Than to have to live through a sequence of events acknowledged
In advance in order to get to a primitive statement. And the mind
Is the beach on which the rocks pop up, just a neutral
Support for them in their indignity. They explain
The trials of our age, cleansing it of toxic

Side-effects as it passes through their system.
Reality. Explained. And for seconds
We live in the same body, are a sibling again.

I think all games and disciplines are contained here,
Painting, as they go, dots and asterisks that
We force into meanings that don't concern us
And so leave us behind. But there are no fractions, the world
   is an integer
Like us, and like us it can neither stand wholly apart nor disappear.
When one is young it seems like a very strange and safe place,
But now that I have changed it feels merely odd, cold
And full of interest. The sofa that was once a seat
Puzzles no longer, while the sweet conversation that occurs
At regular intervals throughout the years is like a collie
One never outgrows. And it happens to you
In this room, it is here, and we can never
Eat of the experience. It drags us down. Much later on
You thought you perceived a purpose in the game at the moment
Another player broke one of the rules; it seemed
A module for the wind, something in which you lose yourself
And are not lost, and then it pleases you to play another day
When outside conditions have changed and only the game
Is fast, perplexed and true, as it comes to have seemed.

Yet one does know why. The covenant we entered
Bears down on us, some are ensnared, and the right way,
It turns out, is the one that goes straight through the house
And out the back. By so many systems
As we are involved in, by just so many
Are we set free on an ocean of language that comes to be
Part of us, as though we would ever get away.
The sky is bright and very wide, and the waves talk to us,

Preparing dreams we'll have to live with and use. The day will come
When we'll have to. But for now
They're useless, more trees in a landscape of trees.

I hadn't expected a glance to be that direct, coming from a sculpture
Of moments, thoughts added on. And I had kept it
Only as a reminder, not out of love. In time I moved on
To become its other side, and then, gentle, anxious, I became as
a parent
To those scenes lifted from "real life." There was the quiet time
In the supermarket, and the pieces
Of other people's lives as they sashayed or tramped past
My own section of a corridor, not pausing
In many cases to wonder where they were—maybe they even knew.
True, those things or moments of which one
Finds oneself an enthusiast, a promoter, are few,
But they last well,
Yielding up their appearances for form
Much later than the others. Forgetting about "love"
For a moment puts one miles ahead, on the steppe or desert
Whose precise distance as it feels I
Want to emphasize and estimate. Because
We will all have to walk back this way
A second time, and not to know it then, not
To number each straggling piece of sagebrush
Is to sleep before evening, and well into the night
That always coaxes us out, smooths out our troubles and puts us back
to bed again.

All those days had a dumb clarity that was about getting out
Into a remembered environment. The headlines and economy
Would refresh for a moment as you look back over the heap
Of rusted box-springs with water under them, and then,

Like sliding up to a door or a peephole a tremendous advantage
Would burst like a bubble. Toys as solemn and knotted as books
Assert themselves first, leading down through a delicate landscape
Of reminders to be better next time to a damp place on my hip,
And this would spell out a warm business letter urging us
All to return to our senses, to the matter of the day
That was ending now. And no special sense of decline ensued
But perhaps a few moments of music of such tact and weariness
That one awakens with a new sense of purpose: more things to be done
And the just-sufficient tools to begin doing them
While awaiting further orders that must materialize soon
Whether in the sand-pit with frightened chickens running around
Or on a large table in a house deep in the country with messages
Pinned to the walls and a sense of plainness quite unlike
Any other waiting. I am prepared to deal with this
While putting together notes related to the question of love
For the many, for two people at once, and for myself
In a time of need unlike those that have arisen so far.
And some day perhaps the discussion that has to come
In order for us to start feeling any of it before we even
Start to think about it will arrive in a new weather
Nobody can imagine but which will happen just as the ages
Have happened without causing total consternation,
Will take place in a night, long before sleep and the love
That comes then, breathing mystery back into all the sterile
Living that had to lead up to it. Moments as clear as water
Splashing on a rock in the sun, though in darkness, and then
Sleep has to affirm it and the body is fresh again,
For the trials and dangerous situations that any love,
However well-meaning, has to use as terms in the argument
That is the reflexive play of our living and being lost
And then changed again, a harmless fantasy that must grow
Progressively serious, and soon state its case succinctly

And dangerously, and we sit down to the table again
Noting the grain of the wood this time and how it pushes through
The pad we are writing on and becomes part of what is written.
Not until it starts to stink does the inevitable happen.

Moving on we approached the top
Of the thing, only it was dark and no one could see,
Only somebody said it was a miracle we had gotten past the
Previous phase, now faced with each other's conflicting
Wishes and the hope for a certain peace, so this would be
Our box and we would stay in it for as long
As we found it comfortable, for the broken desires
Inside were as nothing to the steeply shelving terrain outside,
And morning would arrange everything. So my first impulse
Came, stayed awhile, and left, leaving behind
Nothing of itself, no whisper. The days now move
From left to right and back across this stage and no one
Notices anything unusual. Meanwhile I have turned back
Into that dream of rubble that was the city of our starting out.
No one advises me; the great tenuous clouds of the desert
Sky visit it and they barely touch, so pleasing in the
Immense solitude are the tracks of those who wander and continue
On their route, certain that day will end soon and that night will
then fall.

But behind what looks like heaps of slag the peril
Consists in explaining everything too evenly. Those
Suffering from the blahs are unlikely to notice that the topic
Of today's lecture doesn't exist yet, and in their trauma
Will become one with the vast praying audience as it sways and bends
To the rhythm of an almost inaudible piccolo. And when
It is flushed out, the object of all this meditation will not
Infrequently turn out to be a mere footnote to the great chain

That manages only with difficulty to connect earth and sky together.
Are comments like ours really needed? Of course, heaven is nice
About it, not saying anything, but we, when we come away
As children leaving school at four in the afternoon, can we
Hold our heads up and face the night's homework? No, the
Divine tolerance we seem to feel is actually in short supply,
And those moving forward toward us from the other end of the bridge
Are defending, not welcoming us to, the place of power,
A hill ringed with low, ridgelike fortifications. But when
Somebody better prepared crosses over, he or she will get the same
Cold reception. And so because it is impossible to believe
That anyone lives there, it is we who shall be homeless, outdoors
At the end. And we won't quite know what to do about it.
It's mind-boggling, actually. Each of us must try to concentrate
On some detail or other of their armor: somber, blood-red plumes
Floating over curved blue steel; the ribbed velvet stomacher
And its more social implications. Hurry to deal with the sting
Of added meaning, hurry to fend it off. Your lessons
Will become the ground of which we are made
And shall look back on, for awhile. Life was pleasant there.
And though we made it all up, it could still happen to us again.
Only then, watch out. The burden of proof of the implausible
Picaresque tale, boxes within boxes, will be yours
Next time round. And nobody is going to like your ending.

We had, though, a feeling of security
But we weren't aware of it then: that's
How secure we were. Now, in the dungeon of Better Living,
It seems we may be called back and interrogated about it
Which would be unfortunate, since only the absence of memory
Animates us as we walk briskly back and forth
At one with the soulless, restless crowd on the somber avenue.
Is there something new to see, to speculate on? Dunno, better

Stand back until something comes along to explain it,
This curious lack of anxiety that begins to gnaw
At one. Did it come because happiness hardened everything
In its fire, and so the forms cannot die, like a ruined
Fort too strong to be pulled down? And something like pale
Alpine flowers still flourishes there:
Some reminder that can never be anything more than that,
Yet its balm cares about something, we cannot be really naked
Having this explanation. So a reflected image of oneself
Manages to stay alive through the darkest times, a period
Of unprecedented frost, during which we get up each morning
And go about our business as usual.

And though there are some who leave regularly
For the patchwork landscape of childhood, north of here,
Our own kind of stiff standing around, waiting helplessly
And mechanically for instructions that never come, suits the space
Of our intense, uncommunicated speculation, marries
The still life of crushed, red fruit in the sky and tames it
For observation purposes. One is almost content
To be with people then, to read their names and summon
Greetings and speculation, or even nonsense syllables and
Diagrams from those who appear so brilliantly at ease
In the atmosphere we made by getting rid of most amenities
In the interests of a bare, strictly patterned life that apparently
Has charms we weren't even conscious of, which is
All to the good, except that it fumbles the premise
We put by, saving it for a later phase of intelligence, and now
We are living on it, ready to grow and make mistakes again,
Still standing on one leg while emerging continually
Into an inexpressive void, the blighted fields
Of a kiss, the rope of a random, unfortunate
Observation still around our necks though we thought we

Had cast it off in a novel that has somehow gotten stuck
To our lives, battening on us. A sad condition
To see us in, yet anybody
Will realize that he or she has made those same mistakes,
Memorized those same lists in the due course of the process
Being served on you now. Acres of bushes, treetops;
Orchards where the quince and apple seem to come and go
Mysteriously over long periods of time; waterfalls
And what they conceal, including what comes after—roads
  and roadways
Paved for the gently probing, transient automobile;
Farragoes of flowers; everything, in short,
That makes this explicit earth what it appears to be in our
Glassiest moments when a canoe shoots out from under some foliage
Into the river and finds it calm, not all that exciting but above all
Nothing to be afraid of, celebrates us
And what we have made of it.

Not something so very strange, but then seeming ordinary
Is strange too. Only the way we feel about the everything
And not the feeling itself is strange, strange to us, who live
And want to go on living under the same myopic stars we have known
Since childhood, when, looking out a window, we saw them
And immediately liked them.

And we can get back to that raw state
Of feeling, so long deemed
Inconsequential and therefore appropriate to our later musings
About religion, about migrations. What is restored
Becomes stronger than the loss as it is remembered;
Is a new, separate life of its own. A new color. Seriously blue.
Unquestioning. Acidly sweet. Must we then pick up the pieces
(But what are the pieces, if not separate puzzles themselves,

And meanwhile rain abrades the window?) and move to a central
  clearinghouse
Somewhere in Iowa, far from the distant bells and thunderclaps that
Make this environment pliant and distinct? Nobody
Asked me to stay here, at least if they did I forgot, but I can
Hear the dust at the pores of the wood, and know then
The possibility of something more liberated and gracious
Though not of this time. Failing
That there are the books we haven't read, and just beyond them
A landscape stippled by frequent glacial interventions
That holds so well to its lunette one wants to keep it but we must
Go on despising it until that day when environment
Finally reads as a necessary but still vindictive opposition
To all caring, all explaining. Your finger traces a
Bleeding violet line down the columns of an old directory and to
  this spongy
State of talking things out a glass exclamation point opposes
A discrete claim: forewarned. So the voluminous past
Accepts, recycles our claims to present consideration
And the urban landscape is once again untroubled, smooth
As wax. As soon as the oddity is flushed out
It becomes monumental and anxious once again, looking
Down on our lives as from a baroque pinnacle and not the
Mosquito that was here twenty minutes ago.
The past absconds
With our fortunes just as we were rounding a major
Bend in the swollen river; not to see ahead
Becomes the only predicament when what
Might be sunken there is mentioned only
In crabbed allusions but will be back tomorrow.

It takes only a minute revision, and see—the thing
Is there in all its interested variegatedness,

With prospects and walks curling away, never to be followed,
A civilized concern, a never being alone.
Later on you'll have doubts about how it
Actually was, and certain greetings will remain totally forgotten,
As water forgets a dam once it's over it. But at this moment
A spirit of independence reigns. Quietude
To get out and do things in, and a rush back to the house
When evening turns up, and not a moment too soon.
Headhunters and jackals mingle with the viburnum
And hollyhocks outside, and it all adds up, pointedly,
To something one didn't quite admit feeling uneasy about, but now
That it's all out in the open, like a successful fire
Burning in a fireplace, really there's no cause for alarm.
For even when hours and days go by in silence and the phone
Never rings, and widely spaced drops of water
Fall from the eaves, nothing is any longer a secret
And one can live alone rejoicing in this:
That the years of war are far off in the past or the future,
That memory contains everything. And you see slipping down a
  hallway
The past self you decided not to have anything to do with any more
And it is a more comfortable you, dishonest perhaps,
But alive. Wanting you to know what you're losing.
And still the machinery of the great exegesis is only beginning
To groan and hum. There are moments like this one
That are almost silent, so that bird-watchers like us
Can come, and stay awhile, reflecting on shades of difference
In past performances, and move on refreshed.

But always and sometimes questioning the old modes
And the new wondering, the poem, growing up through the floor,
Standing tall in tubers, invading and smashing the ritual
Parlor, demands to be met on its own terms now,

Now that the preliminary negotiations are at last over.
You could be lying on the floor,
Or not have time for too much of any one thing,
Yet you know the song quickens in the bones
Of your neck, in your heel, and there is no point
In looking out over the yard where tractors run,
The empty space in the endless continuum
Of time has come up: the space that can be filled only by you.
And I had thought about the roadblocks, wondered
Why they were less frequent, wondered what progress the blizzard
Might have been making a certain distance back there,
But it was not enough to save me from choosing
Myself now, from being the place I have to get to
Before nightfall and under the shelter of trees
It is true but also without knowing out there in the dark,

Being alone at the center of a moan that did not issue from me
And is pulling me back toward old forms of address
I know I have already lived through, but they are strong again,
And big to fill the exotic spaces that arguing left.

So all the slightly more than young
Get moved up whether they like it or not, and only
The very old or the very young have any say in the matter,
Whether they are a train or a boat or just a road leading
Across a plain, from nowhere to nowhere. Later on
A record of the many voices of the middle-young will be issued
And found to be surprisingly original. That can't concern us,
However, because now there isn't space enough,
Not enough dimension to guarantee any kind of encounter
The stage-set it requires at the very least in order to burrow
Profitably through history and come out having something to say,
Even just one word with a slightly different intonation

To cause it to stand out from the backing of neatly invented
Chronicles of things men have said and done, like an English horn,
And then to sigh, to faint back
Into all our imaginings, dark
And viewless as they are,
Windows painted over with black paint but
We can sufficiently imagine, so much is admitted, what
Might be going on out there and even play some part
In the ordering of it all into lengths of final night,
Of dim play, of love that at lasts oozes through the seams
In the cement, suppurates, subsumes
All the other business of living and dying, the orderly
Ceremonials and handling of estates,
Checking what does not appear normal and drawing together
All the rest into the report that will finally be made
On a day when it does not appear that there is anything to receive it
Properly and we wonder whether we too are gone,
Buried in our love,
The love that defined us only for a little while,
And when it strolls back a few paces, to get another view,
Fears that it may have encountered eternity in the meantime.
And as the luckless describe love in glowing terms to strangers
In taverns, and the seemingly blessed may be unaware of having
  lost it,
So always there is a small remnant
Whose lives are congruent with their souls
And who ever afterward know no mystery in it,
The cimmerian moment in which all lives, all destinies
And incompleted destinies were swamped
As though by a giant wave that picks itself up
Out of a calm sea and retreats again into nowhere
Once its damage is done.
And what to say about those series

Of infrequent pellucid moments in which
One reads inscribed as though upon an empty page
The strangeness of all those contacts from the time they erupt
Soundlessly on the horizon and in a moment are upon you
Like a stranger on a snowmobile
But of which nothing can be known or written, only
That they passed this way? That to be bound over
To love in the dark, like Psyche, will somehow
Fill the sheaves of pages with a spidery, Spencerian hand
When all that will be necessary will be to go away
For a few minutes in order to return and find the work completed?
And so it is the only way
That love determines us, and we look the same
To others when they happen in afterwards, and cannot even know
We have changed, so massive in our difference
We are, like a new day that looks and cannot be the same
As those we used to reckon with, and so start
On our inane rounds again too dumb to profit from past
Mistakes—that's how different we are!

But once we have finished being interrupted
There is no longer any population to tell us how the gods
Had wanted it—only—so the story runs—a vast forest
With almost nobody in it. Your wants
Are still halfheartedly administered to; sometimes there is milk
And sometimes not, but a ladder of hilarious applause
No longer leads up to it. Instead, there's that cement barrier.
The forest ranger was nice, but warning us away,
Reminded you how other worlds can as easily take root
Like dandelions, in no time. There's no one here now
But émigrés, with abandoned skills, so near
To the surface of the water you can touch them through it.
It's they can tell you how love came and went

And how it keeps coming and going, ever disconcerting,
Even through the topiary trash of the present,
Its undoing, and smiles and seems to recognize no one.
It's all attitudinizing, maybe, images reflected off
Some mirrored surface we cannot see, and they seem both solid
As a suburban home and graceful phantasms, at ease
In any testing climate you may contrive. But surely
The slightly sunken memory that remains, accretes, is proof
That there were doings, yet no one admits to having heard
Even of these. You pass through lawns on the way to it; it's late
Even though the light is strongly yellow; and are heard
Commenting on how hard it is to get anybody to do anything
Any more; suddenly your name is remembered at the end—
It's there, on the list, was there all along
But now is too defunct to cope
Which may be better in the long run: we'll hear of
Other names, and know we don't want them, but that love
Was somehow given out to one of them by mistake,
Not utterly lost. Boyish, slipping past high school
Into the early forties, disingenuous though, yet all
The buds of this early spring won't open, which is surprising,
He says. It isn't likely to get any warmer than it is now.
In today's mainstream one mistakes him, sincerely, for someone else;
He passed on slowly and turns a corner. One can't say
He was gone before you knew it, yet something of that, some tepid
Challenge that was never taken up and disappeared forever,
Surrounds him. Love is after all for the privileged.

But there is something else—call it a consistent eventfulness,
A common appreciation of the way things have of enfolding
When your attention is distracted for a moment, and then
It's all bumps and history, as though this crusted surface
Had always been around, didn't just happen to come into being

A short time ago. The scarred afternoon is unfortunate
Perhaps, but as they come to see each other dimly
And for the first time, an internal romance
Of the situation rises in these human beings like sap
And they can at last know the fun of not having it all but
Having instead a keen appreciation of the ways in which it
Underachieves as well as rages: an appetite,
For want of a better word. In darkess and silence.

In the wind, it is living. What were the interruptions that
Led us here and then shanghaied us if not sincere attempts to
Understand and so desire another person, it doesn't
Matter which one, and then, self-abandoned, to build ourselves
So as to desire him fully, and at the last moment be
Taken aback at such luck: the feeling, invisible but alert.
On that clear February evening thirty-three years ago it seemed
A tapestry of living sounds shading to colors, and today
On this brick stump of an office building the colors are shaggy
Again, are at last what they once were, proving
They haven't changed: you have done that,
Not they. All that remains is to get to know them,
Like a twin brother from whom you were separated at birth
For whom the factory sounds now resonate in an uplifting
Sunset of your own choosing and fabrication, a rousing
Anthem to perpendicularity and the perennial exponential
Narration to cause everything to happen by evoking it
Within the framework of shared boredom and shared responsibilities.
Cheerful ads told us it was all going to be OK,
That the superstitions would do it all for you. But today
It's bigger and looser. People are not out to get you
And yet the walkways look dangerous. The smile slowly soured.
Still, coming home through all this
And realizing its vastness does add something to its dimension:

Teachers would never have stood for this. Which is why
Being tall and shy, you can still stand up more clearly
To the definition of what you are. You are not a sadist
But must only trust in the dismantling of that definition
Some day when names are being removed from things, when
all attributes
Are sinking in the maelstrom of de-definition like spars.
You must then come up with something to say,
Anything, as long as it's no more than five minutes long,
And in the interval you shall have been washed. It's that easy.
But meanwhile, I know, stone tenements are still hoarding
The shadow that is mine; there is nothing to admit to,
No one to confess to. This period goes on for quite a few years
But as though along a low fence by a sidewalk. Then brandishes
New definitions in its fists, but these are evidently false
And get thrown out of court. Next you're on your own
In an old film about two guys walking across the United States.
The love that comes after will be richly satisfying,
Like rain on the desert, calling unimaginable diplomacy into being
Until you thought you should get off here, maybe this stop
Was yours. And then it all happens blindingly, over and over
In a continuous, vivid present that wasn't there before.
No need to make up stories at this juncture, everybody
Likes a joke and they find yours funny. And then it's just
Two giant steps down to the big needing and feeling
That is yours to grow in. Not grow old, the
Magic present still insists on being itself,
But to play in. To live and be lived by
And in this way bring all things to the sensible conclusion
Dreamed into their beginnings, and to arrive at the end.

Simultaneously in an area the size of West Virginia
The opposing view is climbing toward heaven: how swiftly

It rises! How slender the packed silver mass spiraling
Into further thinness, into what can only be called excess,
It seems, now. And anyway it sounds better in translation
Which is the only language you will read it in:
"I was lost, but seemed to be coming home,
Through quincunxes of apple trees, but ever
As I drew closer, as in Zeno's paradox, the mirage
Of home withdrew and regrouped a little farther off.
I could see white curtains fluttering at the windows
And in the garden under a big brass-tinted apple tree
The old man had removed his hat and was gazing at the grass
As though in sorrow, sorrow for what I had done.
Realizing it was now or never, I lurched
With one supreme last effort out of the dream
Onto the couch-grass behind the little red-painted palings:
I was here! But it all seemed so lonesome. I was welcomed
Without enthusiasm. My room had been kept as it was
But the windows were closed, there was a smell of a closed room.
And though I have been free ever since
To browse at will through my appetites, lingering
Over one that seemed special, the lamplight
Can never replace the sad light of early morning
Of the day I left, convinced (as indeed I am today)
Of the logic of my search, yet all unprepared
To look into the practical aspects, the whys and wherefores,
And so never know, eventually, whether I have accomplished
My end, or merely returned, another leaf that falls."
One must be firm not to be taken in by the histrionics
And even more by the rigorous logic with which the enemy
Deploys his message like iron trenches under ground
That rise here and there in blunt, undulating shapes.
And once you have told someone that none of it frightens you
There is still the breached sense of your own being

To live with, to somehow nurse back to plenitude:
Yet it never again has that hidden abundance,
That relaxed, joyous well-being with which
In other times it frolicked along roads, making
The best of ignorance and unconscious, innocent selfishness,
The spirit that was to occupy those times
Now transposed, sunk too deep in its own reflection
For memory. The eager calm of every day.
But in the end the dark stuff, the odd quick attack
Followed by periods of silence that get shorter and shorter
Resolves the subjective-versus-objective approach by undoing
The complications of our planet, its climate, its sonatinas
And stories, its patches of hard ugly snow waiting around
For spring to melt them. And it keeps some memories of the
 troubled
Beginning-to-be-resolved period even in the timely first inkling
Of maturity in March, "when night and day grow equal," but even
More in the solemn peach-harvest that happens some months later
After differing periods of goofing-off and explosive laughter.
To be always articulating these preludes, there seems to be no
Sense in it, if it is going to be perpetually five o'clock
With the colors of the bricks seeping more and more bloodlike
 through the tan
Of trees, and then only to blacken. But it says more
About us. When they finally come
With much laborious jangling of keys to unlock your cell
You can tell them yourself what it is,
Who you are, and how you happened to turn out this way,
And how they made you, for better or for worse, what you are now,
And how you seem to be, neither humble nor proud, *frei aber einsam.*

And should anyone question the viability of this process
You can point to the accessible result. Not like a great victory

That tirelessly sweeps over mankind again and again at the end
Of each era, presuming you can locate it, for the greater good
Of history, though you are not the first person to confuse
Its solicitation with something like scorn, but the slow polishing
Of an infinitely tiny cage big enough to hold all the dispiritedness,
Contempt, and incorrect conclusions based on false premises that now
Slow you down but by that time, enchaliced, will sound attentive,
Tonic even, an antidote to badly reasoned desiring: footfalls
Of the police approaching gingerly through the soft spring air.

At Pine Creek imitation the sky was no nearer. The difference
Was microtones, a seasoning between living and gestures.
It emerged as a rather stiff impression
Of all things. Not that there aren't those glad to have
A useful record like this to add to the collection
In the portfolio. But beyond just needing where is the need
To carry heaven around in one's breast-pocket? To satisfy
The hunger of millions with something more substantial than
  good wishes
And still withhold the final reassurance? So you see these
Days each with its disarming set of images and attitudes
Are beneficial perhaps but only after the last one
In every series has disappeared, down the road, forever, at night.

It would be cockier to ask of heaven just what is this present
Of an old dishpan you bestowed on me? Can I get out the door
With it, now that so many old enmities and flirtations have shrunk
To little more than fine print in the contexts of lives and so much
New ground is coming undone, shaken out like a scarf or a
  handkerchief
From this window that dominates everything perhaps a little too much?
In falling we should note the protective rush of air past us
And then pray for some day after the war to cull each of

The limited set of reflections we were given at the beginning
To try to make a fortune out of. Only then will some kind of
radical stance
Have had some meaning, and for itself, not for us who lie gasping
On slopes never having had the nerve to trust just us, to go out
with us
Not fearing some solemn overseer in the breath from the treetops.

And that that game-plan and the love we have been given for nothing
In particular should coincide—no, it is not yet time to think
these things.
In vain would one try to peel off that love from the object it fits
So nicely, now, remembering it will have to be some day. You
Might as well offer it to your neighbor, the first one you meet,
or throw
It away entirely, as plan to unlock on such and such a date
The door to this forest that has been your total upbringing.
No one expects it, and thus
Flares are launched out over the late disturbed landscape
Of items written down only to be forgotten once more, forever
this time.

And already the sky is getting to be less salmon-colored,
The black clouds more meaningless (otter-shaped at first;
Now, as they retreat into incertitude, mere fins)
And perhaps it's too late for anything like the overhaul
That seemed called for, earlier, but whose initiative
Was it after all? I mean I don't mind staying here
A little longer, sitting quietly under a tree, if all this
Is going to clear up by itself anyway.

There is no indication this will happen,
But I don't mind. I feel at peace with the parts of myself

That questioned this other, easygoing side, chafed it
To a knotted rope of guesswork looming out of storms
And darkness and proceeding on its way into nowhere
Barely muttering. Always, a few errands
Summon us periodically from the room of our forethought
And that is a good thing. And such attentiveness
Besides! Almost more than anybody could bring to anything,
But we managed it, and with a good grace, too. Nobody
Is going to hold *that* against us. But since you bring up the
  question
I will say I am not unhappy to place myself entirely
At your disposal temporarily. Much that had drained out of
  living
Returns, in those moments, mounting the little capillaries
Of polite questions and seeming concern. I want it back.

And though that other question that I asked and can't
Remember any more is going to move still farther upward, casting
Its shadow enormously over where I remain, I can't see it.
Enough to know that I shall have answered for myself soon,
Be led away for further questioning and later returned
To the amazingly quiet room in which all my life has been spent.
It comes and goes; the walls, like veils, are never the same,
Yet the thirst remains identical, always to be entertained
And marveled at. And it is finally we who break it off,
Speed the departing guest, lest any question remain
Unasked, and thereby unanswered. Please, it almost
Seems to say, take me with you, I'm old enough. Exactly.
And so each of us has to remain alone, conscious of each other
Until the day when war absolves us of our differences. We'll
Stay in touch. So they have it, all the time. But all was strange.

A NOTE ABOUT THE AUTHOR

John Ashbery is the author of fifteen books of poetry, including *April Galleons*, *Flow Chart*, and *Hotel Lautréamont*, and a volume of art criticism, *Reported Sightings*. His *Self-Portrait in a Convex Mirror* received the Pulitzer Prize for poetry, as well as the National Book Critics Circle Award and the National Book Award. He has been named a Guggenheim Fellow and a MacArthur Fellow, and is a chancellor of the Academy of American Poets. In 1989–1990 he was Charles Eliot Norton Professor of Poetry at Harvard. He is currently Charles P. Stevenson, Jr., Professor of Literature at Bard College.

Houseboat Days:
Grateful acknowledgment is made to the following publications, in which these poems originally appeared: *American Poetry Review*: "Variant," "The Couple in the Next Room," "Lost and Found and Lost Again," and "Saying It to Keep It from Happening"; *Antaeus*: "Crazy Weather" and "Bird's-Eye View of the Tool and Die Co."; *Chicago Review*: "All Kinds of Caresses" and "The Thief of Poetry"; *Denver Quarterly*: "Unctuous Platitudes" and "On the Towpath"; *Georgia Review*: "Loving Mad Tom" and "Whether It Exists"; *New York Review of Books*: "Valentine," "Houseboat Days," "Street Musicians," "The Gazing Grain," "Wet Casements," and "Friends"; *The New Yorker*: "Melodic Trains," "Collective Dawns," "The Lament upon the Waters," and "The Wrong Kind of Insurance"; *Poetry*: "The Ice-Cream Wars," "Blue Sonata," "Syringa," and "Fantasia on 'The Nut-Brown Maid' "; *Roof*: "Two Deaths"; *The Scotsman*: "The Explanation"; *Spectator*: "And *Ut Pictura Poesis* Is Her Name"; *Sun*: "And Others, Vaguer Presences"; *Times Literary Supplement*: "Business Personals" and "Daffy Duck in Hollywood"; *Vanderbilt Poetry Review*: "What Is Poetry"; *Yale French Studies*: "Drame Bourgeois"; *Z*: "The Other Tradition" and "Wooden Buildings."

"The Serious Doll" was first published by the Kermani Press. "Pyrography" was commissioned by the U.S. Department of the Interior for its Bicentennial exhibition, "America 1976," and first appeared in the exhibition catalog published by the Hereward Lester Cooke Foundation.

Shadow Train:
Grateful acknowledgment is made to the following publications in which some of these poems originally appeared: *Issues* (Brown University): "Catalpas"; *New York Review of Books*: "Qualm" and "Caesura"; *The New Yorker*: "The Pursuit of Happiness"; *Times Literary Supplement*: "Paradoxes and Oxymorons," "Or in My Throat," and "A Pace with Sullen Death"; *Yale Review*: "Tide Music" and "Unusual Precautions"; *Zero*: "Night Life" and "But Not That One."

A Wave:
Acknowledgment is made to the following publications, in which some of the poems in this book originally appeared: *American Poetry Review*: "A Wave"; *Conjunction*: "When the Sun Went Down," "A Fly," "I See, Said the Blind Man, as He Put Down His Hammer and Saw," "Destiny Waltz," "Problems," and "They Like"; *Grand Street*: "But What Is the Reader to Make of This?" "Purists Will Object," and "Darlene's Hospital"; *Mothers of Mud*: "Edition Peters, Leipzig"; *New York Arts Journal*: "Cups with Broken Handles" and "The Path to the White Moon"; *New York Review of Books*: "Landscape (After Baudelaire)" and "More Pleasant Adventures"; *The New Yorker*: "At North Farm," "Down by the Station Early in the Morning," "Proust's Questionnaire," "The Ongoing Story," and "Never Seek to Tell Thy Love"; *Paris Review*: "Rain Moving In"; *Rolling Stone*: "Staffage"; *Sulphur*: "37 Haiku," "Haibun (1–6)," and "So Many Lives"; *Times Literary Supplement*: "Just Walking Around," "The Songs We Know Best," "Thank You for Not Cooperating," and "Trefoil"; *Vanity Fair*: "Around the Rough and Rugged Rocks the Ragged Rascal Rudely Ran"; *Virginia Quarterly Review*: "The Lonedale Operator."

"Variation on a Noel," "The Songs We Know Best," "The Lonedale Operator," and "Whatever It Is, Wherever You Are" appear in *Apparitions*, a limited-edition anthology published by Lord John Press. "Description of a Masque" appears in *Contemporary American Fiction*, an anthology published by Sun & Moon Press.

Grateful acknowledgment is made to the following for permission to reprint copyrighted material:

EMI Music Company: Portions of lyrics from the song "Sentimental Journey," by Les Brown and Benjamin Homer. Used by permission of Morley Music, % Colgems EMI Music, Inc., Hollywood, California. All rights reserved.

Oxford University Press, England: A selection from "When We Dead Awaken," by Henrik Ibsen, from *The Oxford Ibsen*, Vol. VIII.